A Very Darcy Christmas
A Pride and Prejudice Variation

Victoria Kincaid

ISBN: 978-0-9975530-4-8

This book is dedicated to my mother who showed me the value of believing in myself

Chapter One

"Mrs. Darcy, there are people downstairs in the entrance hall who say they are your parents."

Disdain dripped off every syllable Giles uttered. Elizabeth pretended not to notice. Every day Pemberley's butler demonstrated that he did not approve of the upstart country lass his master had married. In the months since William had brought her home as his bride, Giles's friendliest tone of voice could be described as frosty. On the other hand, Mrs. Reynolds, the housekeeper, and the majority of the other staff had been most welcoming.

Elizabeth rushed to her feet. Her parents should be safely ensconced at Longbourn for the Christmas season. *What could have brought them to Pemberley unannounced?*

She hurried from her sitting room and followed Giles down the grand front staircase, her heart contracting with every step as she imagined what kinds of evil might have befallen her family. Her mother and father were indeed standing in the hall.

Their rumpled, travel-worn attire contrasted noticeably with the grandeur of the room. The inhabitants of Pemberley called it the marble hall because of the black and white marble squares covering the floor as well as the classical statues set in niches along the walls.

It was an impressive room, meant to stir amazement in Pemberley's newly arrived visitors, and from the expressions on her parents' faces, it was having the desired effect. Elizabeth had been duly impressed when she had first arrived at Pemberley, but now the room reminded her of a mausoleum, grand and cold and forbidding. She and Mrs. Reynolds had recently finished decorating the room with holly, evergreen boughs, ivy, and mistletoe for the yuletide season. The greens softened the room's sharp edges, but it was only slightly more welcoming.

Her father's careworn face relaxed into a smile when he saw her as if her presence made the unfamiliar surroundings more bearable. *He does not seem overly alarmed; perhaps the situation is not dire.* However, the moment her mother noticed Elizabeth, she commenced fluttering her hands and breathing rapidly as if she had experienced a terrible shock.

In other words, everything was quite normal.

Before Elizabeth could open her mouth, her mother launched into a torrent of complaints. "Oh, my dearest Lizzy! You do not know how we have suffered. The ruts in the road and the quality of the coaching inns!

And there was a most disturbing odor in Lambton when we traveled through."

Standing by the ornately carved front door, Giles watched this performance with a pinched mouth and lifted chin that left no doubt as to his opinion of the Bennets.

The best Elizabeth could do was to treat her mother's shrieking as if she spoke in a normal conversational tone. She embraced both of her parents. "This is a surprise! I did not expect to see you so soon. Is something wrong?" She searched their faces for signs of agitation. Had something happened to one of her sisters?

"Everything is well," her father assured her.

Mrs. Bennet gaped at her husband. "How can you say that, Mr. Bennet, when we have heard the most frightful news imaginable?"

Fear gripped Elizabeth's chest. "What has happened?"

Her mother drew herself up to her full height. "Meryton is about to be invaded!"

"It is?"

Her mother's head nodded vigorously. "Mrs. Long was the first one to rouse my suspicions." Now she lowered her voice. "There have been a great many *strange men* visiting Meryton—speaking in French accents!"

Mr. Bennet rolled his eyes. "Fanny, I explained that both of the men are laborers from Ireland. They speak with *Irish* accents."

Mrs. Bennet put her hands on her hips. "And how would you know a French accent from an Irish one? Mrs. Long met a Frenchman when she was one and twenty. She knows how they sound!"

"Mama—" Elizabeth began.

"But that is not all," her mother continued. "Colonel Forster's regiment had been wintering over in Meryton as before, but then they decamped suddenly. Called away, just like that! I wager they are in Brighton at this moment, preparing to fend off a ferocious French assault."

Elizabeth bit her lip to stifle a smile. "I have read nothing to suggest that in the papers."

"Of course not!" Mrs. Bennet waved her handkerchief dramatically. "The authorities do not wish to stir up alarm. But why else would they have called the regiment away?"

"There *was* political unrest in the North," Mr. Bennet murmured.

"Mrs. Long does not believe it," Mrs. Bennet said with a dismissive nod. "And what is more, *Mr. Long* does not believe it. He was in the militia for a year in his youth and said such orders were highly irregular.

"Fanny—" Mr. Bennet started.

Her words continued unchecked. "An invasion is imminent. Nothing you may say can convince me otherwise." She folded her arms across her chest.

Elizabeth feared this was the truest statement her mother had uttered since arriving.

Mrs. Bennet continued without even taking a breath. "And, of course, Meryton will be one of the French army's first targets."

"Before London?" Elizabeth asked.

"Well, London will be well-defended. Meryton no longer even boasts a militia!" Mrs. Bennet flicked open her fan and vigorously fanned her face. "Mary and Kitty refused to leave Hertfordshire. Even Jane would not listen. But I told your father I was coming to Pemberley. Since it is so much further north, we have much less of a chance of being slaughtered in our beds." She folded her fan again. "How very clever of you to catch the eye of a northern man."

Having never considered this a feature of her marriage to William, Elizabeth did not respond.

"I pray you let us stay here for a while. What say you, Lizzy?"

Elizabeth gave her father a helpless look, not knowing where to start unraveling her mother's convoluted reasoning. Mr. Bennet offered her a defeated shrug. Apparently he had given up on reasoning with his wife.

Well, she could hardly turn away her own parents. Perhaps she could talk sense into her mother during her visit. "Yes, of course, Mama. I am very pleased to see you both!" She smiled at them. "Welcome to Pemberley."

Her father gave her a rather sad smile, but her mother grunted in response. "Now, if you will have them show me to my room. I am greatly fatigued by all this travel!" Now that their immediate fate had been settled, Mrs. Bennet eyed the hall critically. "Oh, Lizzy!" Her hand flew to her mouth. "You have hung greens already!"

"They make the house more festive," Elizabeth replied.

"But it is bad luck to hang greens before Christmas Eve!" Her mother's eyes were round with concern.

"Just a superstition—" her father interjected.

"No, it is not!" Mrs. Bennet exclaimed, wringing her hands. "Mrs. Taylor hung her greens early one year, and the very next day their chickens refused to lay a single egg! She never made that mistake again, I will tell you." She pointed an accusatory finger at Elizabeth. "You have practically begged the French to invade."

Elizabeth rolled her eyes. "I like the greens."

Mrs. Bennet's hands fluttered. "Well, don't blame me when the French invade. I warned you!"

"I promise not to blame you, Mama, if the French invade." Elizabeth gestured to the butler. Perhaps her mother would be more rational after she rested and freshened up. One could only hope. "Giles, I think we can put my parents in the red bedchamber."

Giles's expression could not possibly have been haughtier, but he gave a slight bow and left to summon a maid. As the maid led Mrs. Bennet up the stairs, the older woman warned the wide-eyed girl about the imminent French invasion. Elizabeth and her father fell behind, staying out of earshot.

"I apologize, Lizzy," he said. "Trying to stop her was like trying to halt a runaway carriage. When she declared her intention to visit Pemberley with or without me, I thought my presence might mitigate the damage."

Elizabeth took her father's arm. "I am very pleased to see you both, Papa. And it will provide an opportunity to show you Pemberley."

He smiled gently. "I must confess, that is something I am anticipating with pleasure. What I have seen so far is quite grand."

Elizabeth gave her father's arm another reassuring squeeze, but her spirits sank. With Georgiana visiting Rosings Park for the yuletide season, Elizabeth and William had been anticipating a quiet Christmas celebration by themselves. Since they had arrived at Pemberley after their wedding voyage, Elizabeth's life had been a whirlwind. She had spent much of her time familiarizing herself with the household and the servants, caring for tenants, entertaining neighbors, and performing the many other tasks required of Mrs. Darcy. William had been looking forward to having her to himself over Christmas, and the feeling was very much reciprocated.

Well, Mama and Papa are only two people, Elizabeth reminded herself. *And Papa will happily spend much of his time in the library. Certainly I can find a way to occupy Mama.*

Elizabeth and her father had just reached the top of the stairs when she heard quick footsteps behind them. Glancing over her shoulder, she found one of the footmen rushing toward her, his brow creased with worry. "Madam, Mr. Giles sent me to inform you. Miss Darcy's coach is on the drive!"

Elizabeth blinked. *Georgiana? What was the matter?* Her sister-in-law had planned to visit Rosings Park for at least three more weeks, until Twelfth Night. Although Lady Catherine had initially severed all contact with Pemberley, she had recently insisted on Georgiana's company—no doubt hoping to counteract Elizabeth's pernicious influence. Georgiana had assented in part because she hoped to mend the breach between her brother and her aunt, although William had told her not to bother.

Elizabeth turned to her father. "Papa, I must meet Georgiana's coach. Sally will help with anything you might need, and I shall see you at supper."

Her father patted her hand reassuringly. Elizabeth quickly retreated down the great marble staircase. Georgiana was just entering the house. The slight woman was rumpled from travel, and some of her blonde curls tumbled into her eyes. But Elizabeth was most concerned about the signs of strain around the younger woman's mouth and the tension in her shoulders.

Giles took Georgiana's pelisse and bonnet, and then Elizabeth hurried to embrace her. "Is there trouble, my dear?" Elizabeth asked. "Are you feeling quite well?"

"Yes, my health is good." Georgiana grimaced. "But William was correct. Visiting Rosings was most unpleasant. Aunt Catherine took every opportunity to disparage you and William. In addition, she invited two young men—both distant relatives of hers—to Rosings. It is clear they think they can be my suitors." Elizabeth bit her tongue against a quick retort. *How dare her ladyship ambush Georgiana in such a way?* "It was so uncomfortable."

This was one of the longest speeches Elizabeth had ever heard from Darcy's sister; clearly she was quite disturbed. Elizabeth squeezed Georgiana's hand sympathetically. "I can understand. Were they both so terrible?"

Georgiana sighed, pushing curls from her eyes. "Perhaps not, but I am not prepared to meet suitors, particularly without you and William to give me advice."

Of course. After the Wickham debacle, Georgiana would be reluctant to trust her own judgment about men. Lady Catherine should not have attempted to influence her niece's matrimonial prospects, but obviously she hoped to circumvent William's authority. Elizabeth could think of several things to say about the woman, but she held her tongue.

"I decided to come home. I hope you are not too disappointed with me."

Elizabeth gave her another hug. "Of course not, darling. I am very happy to see you, and William will be as well. He is out visiting tenants but will be home for supper. We would have missed you at Christmas! Oh, and my parents have come to visit from Longbourn as well."

Georgiana gave a gentle smile. "How lovely. We shall be a merry party!"

Yes, thought Elizabeth. *Hopefully my mother will not celebrate Christmas by discussing how we will be murdered in our beds.*

Georgiana gave her sister-in-law another hug. "And you have decorated so nicely for the yule season. Mama never hung greens before Christmas Eve."

Elizabeth smiled despite another reminder of her decorating deficiencies.

Georgiana took her leave and climbed wearily up the stairs toward her bedchamber. Although Elizabeth was pleased to have her sister-in-law home for the yule season, she could not prevent a pang of regret over more loss of privacy. *But it is a big house,* Elizabeth thought as she watched Georgiana disappear up the stairs. *She is merely one more person. We shall hardly notice her.*

Elizabeth had only taken one step toward the stairs when a brisk knock sounded on the door. *Oh no, what now?* Elizabeth fervently prayed for a wayward deliveryman.

Giles hastened to open the door. Elizabeth instantly recognized the tall figure silhouetted against the pale winter sky. "Richard!" she exclaimed.

Colonel Fitzwilliam strode into the hall, beating some of the dust off of his clothing with a pair of riding gloves. "Elizabeth." He gallantly kissed the back of her hand. "I apologize for appearing unexpectedly. But I received a letter from Aunt Catherine complaining that Georgiana left Rosings suddenly."

Elizabeth's brows knit together. "And you came to chastise her?"

He chuckled. "No. I came to congratulate her on her narrow escape." But then his face sobered. "And I wondered what Aunt Catherine had done to disturb my fair cousin."

Privately, Elizabeth believed that both William and Richard perceived Georgiana to be more fragile than she actually was. "You may ask Georgiana that question," Elizabeth said neutrally.

Richard scowled. "So Aunt Catherine is up to something! Blast!" His eyes glanced up the stairs as if he could magically conjure Georgiana with his thoughts.

"You rode all the way from London because of a letter?" Elizabeth asked.

His eyes burned with a peculiar intensity. "I would ride from Spain if Georgiana needed me." Abruptly he blinked, shifting his attention to unbuttoning his great coat. "However, heroic measures were not necessary. I was in Matlock, visiting my family at Edgemont Manor for the Christmas season. I actually accompanied General Burke and his wife; they have long been friends of my family."

Elizabeth's eyes opened wide. She had not known the war hero was a friend of Richard's parents. "Should I have a maid show you to your customary chamber?" she asked.

Richard's easy smile returned. "I will find it myself. Thank you."

"I hope you will join us for dinner," she said. "My parents are also visiting."

"That would be lovely." His eyes wandered around the hall. "My mother would say that hanging greens before Christmas Eve is bad luck, although I think it looks lovely."

Elizabeth simply nodded. *Why must everyone comment on the Christmas greens?*

A second later he was striding up the stairs. Elizabeth heaved a sigh of relief. *This is getting ridiculous.* Their hopes of a cozy Christmas alone were evaporating before her eyes. "We simply have too many relations," she murmured to herself. From his post near the door, Giles gave her a sidelong glance, but Elizabeth returned a sunny smile. She could never show the smallest doubt in front of the butler.

With Mrs. Reynolds busy readying rooms for the new arrivals, Elizabeth determined that it was her responsibility to speak with Cook about additions to their party and alterations to the menu. However, Elizabeth had only taken one step toward the kitchen when a loud, imperious knock reverberated on the door. "Oh no," she groaned. "This is simply too much!"

Giles hastened to throw open the door; to Elizabeth's horror, Lady Catherine swept into the marble hall. Elizabeth prevented a cry of dismay from escaping her lips, but no doubt her expression was less than welcoming.

Lady Catherine was on the arm of a dark-haired, handsome young man in well-tailored clothing. Behind her trailed a small retinue of servants and a scrawny, ginger-haired man in a garish blue coat. He absently carried several stalks of wheat in his right hand.

Elizabeth strode across the hall to greet Lady Catherine with a curtsey. The other woman regarded her coolly. "Miss Elizabeth. I trust you are well?" She examined Elizabeth from head to toe as if no part of her clothing could possibly be acceptable.

"Yes," Elizabeth said through clenched teeth. "And it is Mrs. Darcy now, ma'am. We sent you an announcement of the wedding, but perhaps it went astray."

"Hmph." Lady Catherine sniffed.

"We did not expect your ladyship." There was an understatement. "I understood you were to spend the Christmas season at Rosings Park."

The other woman disengaged her hand from the dark-haired man's arm and stalked around the hall, eyeing everything critically. For once Elizabeth was grateful for Giles's fastidiousness. "And I understood," Lady Catherine said acidly, "that I was to spend the yule season with Georgiana, but she fled Rosings and returned here." She eyed Elizabeth as if she had encouraged such behavior in her sister-in-law.

But Elizabeth was only now understanding the implications of Lady Catherine's presence. "You followed her all the way to Derbyshire?" Elizabeth said faintly.

The other woman regarded Elizabeth haughtily. "I was concerned about her well-being, and I wished to reassure myself that she had arrived safely home."

"I may assure you she is excellent health, so there is no need—"

Lady Catherine interrupted, giving no indication she even noticed Elizabeth was speaking. "And Georgiana barely had time to acquaint herself with Lord Robert, Viscount Barrington"—she gestured to the dark-haired man—"or Mr. Worthy." She indicated the scarecrow-like man, who ignored the glories of the marble hall in favor of examining the wheat in his hand.

Viscount Barrington at least had the grace to appear abashed. "I apologize for imposing on your hospitality," he said to Elizabeth. "My own estate is only a half hour drive from here, so I can just as easily depart in the morning."

Agreeing to this arrangement would make Elizabeth appear to be an ungracious hostess. "No, of course we are pleased to have you stay."

There was a pause while every eye in the hall turned to Mr. Worthy. After several seconds he glanced up from the wheat. "I hope you do not mind hosting me, Mrs. Darcy. You have the most fascinating hybrid here—I found it in the field near the drive..." His attention wandered back to the wheat. Lady Catherine cleared her throat. "Oh, and, of course, I am pleased to make Miss Darcy's acquaintance."

Elizabeth managed to keep a straight face at this declaration, but Lady Catherine's lips tightened slightly. No wonder Georgiana harbored some doubts about this "suitor."

With all of the unexpected visitors so far, Elizabeth had felt an obligation to host them. However, Lady Catherine would present many difficulties. Not only did she bring a large retinue with her, but also her presence would likely disturb Georgiana. Nor had Elizabeth forgotten all of the ungenerous things her ladyship had said the last time they had met. "I am not sure now is the right time for a visit," Elizabeth temporized. "Perhaps if you—"

"We have come all the way from Kent," Lady Catherine declared loudly. "It was quite a long and arduous journey."

Elizabeth blinked rapidly. What was she to say in the face of such a declaration?

The older woman drew herself up to her full height. "I know my *nephew* will be pleased to see me."

Elizabeth rather doubted that assertion, but did she really have the authority to gainsay William's relative? "Of course, you are welcome to stay tonight. I will have some rooms made up." She mustered a smile as she spoke. Maybe William would find some way to dissuade his aunt from staying for the entire holiday season.

She turned to Giles, but before she could utter a word, Lady Catherine gasped. "Holly boughs and evergreens before Christmas Eve! Why would you allow your staff to do such a thing?" She glared down her nose at Elizabeth. "It is horribly bad luck, you know."

"I had not heard that." Elizabeth smiled sweetly at her husband's aunt. She gestured to the butler. "Giles, Lady Catherine, Lord Robert, and Mr. Worthy will need to be shown to guest chambers."

Giles's supercilious expression transformed into a charming smile when he turned to the guests. There was no doubt which people he preferred. "This way, my lady, my lord, Mr. Worthy." He gestured politely up the stairs.

Soon Lady Catherine and her entourage were gone from sight. Elizabeth stood in the marble hall by herself trying to understand what had just happened to her yule season. Thus, she was the only one available to answer the door at the sound of yet another knock. *At this point, I am numb to any more shocks*, she thought as she opened the door.

However, she was immediately proved wrong when she saw who stood on her doorstep.

Lydia threw her arms around Elizabeth. "Lizzy!" Her sister gestured to her husband, George Wickham. "We were visiting George's friends in Lambton when we heard you were entertaining visitors for Christmas—even Mama and Papa! I was so excited. It has been forever since I have seen them!"

Words failed Elizabeth, so she merely opened the door wider to allow the couple to enter.

Chapter Two

Even his horse was tired. Darcy could sense the animal's weariness in the way he plodded along the road back to Pemberley. He had traveled far and wide visiting tenants, inspecting fallow fields, discussing drainage issues with the steward, and performing many other little tasks that were incumbent upon a good landowner. Darcy leaned forward to pat Zeus's neck. "You did a good job today, boy. You have earned some oats and a warm stall."

And I have earned a nice quiet evening reading by the fire—with Elizabeth resting her head on my shoulder. Some of the weariness lifted at this vision. Although Darcy had been eager to marry once Elizabeth had accepted him, he had not realized how wonderful married life could be. He relished tender, quiet moments reading together in the library or animated conversation at dinner as much as any time they spent in bed— although that had a lot to recommend it as well. The thought of Elizabeth at home—waiting for him—filled him with warmth.

The sun had set long ago; Darcy shivered a little despite his greatcoat. He had accomplished many of the tasks on his list today. Life at Pemberley was slow during the winter; he could indulge in some idle time with his new wife.

Darcy sat up a little straighter in the saddle and kicked the horse to a faster pace. Soon they were clip-clopping along the drive toward Pemberley Manor. Darcy handed Zeus's reins over to a groom with instructions to give the stallion some oats.

As he strode toward the front door, he wondered what foods Elizabeth might have ordered for their supper. Soup? Beef? Perhaps a pudding? Since it would be the two of them, perhaps they could have a tray in their sitting room upstairs. That would be quite cozy.

However, an unexpected sight greeted Darcy when he opened the door. Maids were bustling along the upstairs balcony that overlooked the marble hall. Footmen were crossing the checkerboard floor tiles quite purposefully. Giles's deep voice was giving orders in the dining room, although his words were imperceptible. What in blazes was happening?

A footman sprang forward to relieve Darcy of his greatcoat. Before he could ask the man if Elizabeth had sent the whole house into a frenzy of cleaning, he heard the murmur of voices from the saloon.

Could they possibly have guests? No one was expected, but a neighbor might have stopped for a visit. Or his aunt and uncle? Matlock was not too far away. But that would not explain all the activity.

The saloon, a large oval room behind the marble hall, was comfortably appointed with chairs and settees and decorated in the latest fashion. As he entered the room, Darcy was treated to the sight—and sound—of Mrs. Bennet's shrieks.

"It's the French! They here!" She was pointing to Richard on the other side of the room. What was his cousin doing at Pemberley?

Richard actually looked to see if some spy had crept into the room behind him. Then his eyes widened as he realized Mrs. Bennet was accusing him.

"That is my nephew, you ninny," a voice Darcy recognized all too well rang out. His aunt Catherine glared disdainfully at Mrs. Bennet. *Aunt Catherine and Mrs. Bennet in the same room? Surely fate could not be so cruel.*

"He doesn't have a mustache, Mama," chimed in Lydia Wickham. *Oh, Good Lord, it got worse and worse.* "All Frenchmen have mustaches. Everyone knows that."

If Lydia was here, that meant…

"Yes, by all means, Fitzwilliam, I think you should prove you are not a French spy," drawled Wickham from the sideboard where he was helping himself to some of Darcy's best brandy.

Richard advanced menacingly on Wickham, who shrank back against the wall. "I do not need to prove anything to you or anyone," he snarled to the other man.

"He does not *sound* French," Mrs. Bennet admitted. "Perhaps he is Irish."

Mr. Bennet handed his wife a glass. "My dear, here is some of that sherry you like."

A skinny red-haired man was the first one to notice Darcy standing in the shadow of the doorway. "Mr. Darcy?" He bounced enthusiastically from his chair. "I must talk with you, sir! You have a most interesting blight!" The man waved a piece of wheat in Darcy's face, forcing him to take a step back.

"Not now, you fool!" hissed Lady Catherine.

The man blinked at her. "Oh, should we talk about blights over port after dinner?"

Good Lord, has the whole world gone mad?

"William!"

Elizabeth appeared in the doorway, a little more careworn than when he had left her that morning. Some of her hair had escaped and fell over her face. Dark smudges shadowed her eyes. Even so, she was a rock of sanity amidst all of the unexpected chaos—and a balm to his weary soul. He took both of her hands in his and pulled her toward him, giving her a hearty kiss on the lips. When he released her, a faint blush stained her cheeks.

"Really, William!" Aunt Catherine said in her most scandalized voice.

Darcy found it remarkably easy to ignore her. "Did you open a boarding house while I was gone for the day?" he asked Elizabeth with a smile.

Richard chuckled. "I cannot speak for your other guests, but I have no intention of paying for my room and board."

Elizabeth laughed, too. "I apologize that I was not here to welcome you! I wanted to explain the sudden onslaught of guests."

She took him by the arm and walked him out into the marble hall as she explained how they had become inundated with visitors. Darcy did not understand at first why she chose to lead him away from their guests, but by the end of the recitation he did. "…And my parents are here because my mother fears the French will invade Meryton; she thinks being further north will be safer." Elizabeth rolled her eyes. Darcy managed not to laugh.

"I see," he said.

"I apologize that my family took it upon themselves to visit without an invitation," Elizabeth murmured.

"'Tis not your fault." He shook his head, although he could not help but mourn the demise of their quiet Christmas together. None of the guests could be easily persuaded to leave before Twelfth Night, except perhaps Richard—and he was the only one Darcy would keep. It would be rude and inhospitable to invite the others to leave during the Christmas season.

They would weather it with no difficulties, he was sure. Although it was a close call who had the more irritating laugh, Lydia or Mrs. Bennet. And then Wickham on top of that… Darcy's hands clenched into fists.

"We must discover a way to remove Mr. Wickham from the premises," Elizabeth said firmly. "Particularly because Georgiana was among the first of the arrivals. She found Rosings to be overwhelming."

"Or rather Aunt Catherine." Darcy ground his back teeth. "Does Georgiana know of Wickham?"

"I warned her. She claimed to be equal to meeting him, but I could see that it bothered her." She sighed. "I do not believe we can do anything about the man, however. We must feed him and give him a room for the night."

Darcy nodded despite his misgivings. "Very well. I will require him to remove to the Lambton Inn tomorrow."

"Dinner will be served whenever you are ready," Elizabeth said.

He sighed. "Very well, I will go upstairs and change my clothes." But he did not move; instead he stared at the saloon door. "I was only away for a few hours…" he murmured in amazement.

Elizabeth patted his arm. "I know how you feel, my dear."

***

Elizabeth must have given the seating arrangements very careful consideration, Georgiana reflected, taking into account the…peculiarities of the guests at the dinner table. Georgiana herself was near the head of the table, between her brother and Richard, while Mr. Wickham and his wife were near the foot where Elizabeth sat. The man's presence no longer troubled her as much as it once had, but she was pleased to be too far away for conversation.

Richard noticed her surreptitious glance in Mr. Wickham's direction. "Does he bother you? I would happily take him to the kitchen for the rest of the meal."

She shook her head, her lips pressed tightly together. "He does not make me anxious," she assured her cousin. "He is simply unpleasant and irritating, much like a wart."

Richard guffawed and quickly covered his mouth with his napkin. "Clearly your wit has not deserted you, Georgie." He gave her hand a too-brief squeeze. "Your best revenge is to demonstrate that his presence does not concern you—and show how happy you are."

Georgiana could see the wisdom in this approach. "Indeed." As she leaned forward to grasp her wineglass, her eyes happened to catch Mr. Wickham's. He gave her a knowing smirk that was no doubt intended to unsettle her. Georgiana did feel a chill travel down her spine, but she kept her face blank.

With a bit of a smile, she leaned over to Richard and whispered in his ear. "Shall we make the scoundrel self-conscious by laughing about him?"

Richard's eyes darted to the officer, who watched them warily. Her cousin exchanged glances with Georgiana, and they both burst into laughter. She was genuinely amused, knowing that the scoundrel was unaware why they laughed. When she ventured a glance down the table, Mr. Wickham stared fixedly at his plate, but the tips of his ears were red, a sure sign that he noticed their attention.

On the other hand, Aunt Catherine, seated across from Georgiana, shot them both a disapproving glare. As far as she was concerned, excessive merriment was unwelcome at the dinner table. Unfortunately, the gift of her aunt's attention was a double-edged sword. She raised her eyebrows disdainfully at her niece. "My dear, imagine our surprise when you left Rosings Park so abruptly."

All vestiges of mirth fled. Georgiana's eyes lowered to her food, and she took up her utensils. "As I told you before I left Rosings, I found I could not bear to be away from Pemberley during the yuletide season. I have always been here for Christmas."

Georgiana's eyes flickered to William. Was he angry over her precipitous departure from Rosings? His face was impassive, but she saw no shadow of disapproval in his eyes.

"You barely had an opportunity to make the acquaintance of Mr. Worthy or Viscount Barrington." Aunt Catherine gestured to the two men seated on either side of her chair. "The viscount's ancestral estates are here in Derbyshire."

This was at least the fourth time her aunt had relayed that information—as if propinquity would be Georgiana's primary criterion for choosing a husband. "Indeed? How interesting," Georgiana said as she focused on cutting her meat into smaller and smaller pieces. In truth she found Lord Robert intriguing. While Mr. Worthy was impossible in every way, the viscount was handsome and well-spoken. But Georgiana had no opportunities to speak with him alone; her aunt was always present, directing the conversation.

Lord Robert smiled and appeared ready to speak when Mr. Worthy interjected, "My family's land is in Kent. It is very fertile."

William seemed to catch something in his throat and coughed loudly into his napkin.

Mr. Worthy continued, oblivious. "We have implemented all of the latest techniques in crop circulation."

One of William's eyebrows rose. "Crop *rotation?*"

"Exactly!" Mr. Worthy beamed at William as if he were a small child who had solved a mathematics problem rather than a powerful landowner who had corrected the other man's inaccurate language.

William cut his meat rather more forcefully than usual, but he said nothing.

"Mr. Worthy's mother and I are second cousins," Aunt Catherine intoned.

Is that the only reason Aunt Catherine is imposing this man upon me? wondered Georgiana. *She could not possibly believe we would make a good match.*

She would have preferred to familiarize herself with the viscount, but he had become involved in a conversation with Mr. Bennet. Richard was engaged in discourse with Mrs. Wickham. Mr. Worthy, on the other hand, regarded Georgiana like an eager puppy, awaiting her next words. *I really should speak with him.* Under the table she wiped damp palms on her dress. She had never claimed much expertise in the art of making conversation. But Mrs. Annesley had given her advice about it: "You may always ask the other person about his or her life. Everyone loves to talk about himself."

That was the answer. She could ask one question, and then he would do all the talking. "What sorts of crops do you plant on your estate?" she asked him.

The man beamed at her, sitting a little straighter in his chair. "Well, in our north fields we have wheat, although the steward has suggested switching those to corn. That could increase the yield by up to twelve percent. The east fields were fallow last year, but now we have them planted with a heartier variety of potatoes. And then in the west— oh, I should add that one of the east fields is dedicated to barley because my steward thought…"

Half an hour later the occupants of one end of the table were still listening to the fascinating tales of Mr. Worthy's adventures in crop rotation. He spoke with the superior air of someone who condescended to share great pearls of wisdom that others should be grateful to receive. Georgiana cast a sidelong glance at her brother. Although he could usually talk about agriculture for some time, even his eyes were glazing over. Of course, this was a monologue rather than a discussion.

"…Naturally, it required a great deal more irrigation." Mr. Worthy paused to take a breath, but Georgiana had been waiting to pounce on the slightest lull.

"And what do your tenants think about such improvements?" she asked. Surely Mr. Worthy's improvements had created a vast deal more work for them.

"The tenants?" he echoed as if he had never heard the word before.

"Have they been supportive of all the changes?" she asked. Both Richard and William were now watching with avid interest. They must have had the same thought.

"W-why yes—of-of course! I believe so…" he stammered.

In other words, he had never asked them. William always emphasized the importance of working with the tenants and involving them in any major changes on the estate. After all, it was their livelihood.

Mr. Worthy's briefly troubled expression gave way to one of renewed enthusiasm. "Oh, and I neglected to tell you about the new fertilizer we have been experimenting with!" Georgiana cast an imploring look at her aunt, but the older woman's eyes were closed. Good gracious, the man had managed to put her to sleep at the dining table!

This would not do. If Georgiana must tolerate the man's ramblings, then her aunt must suffer as well. She glanced around the table for tools with which to enact a plan. Her eyes fell on a metal cover over a basket of rolls.

Reaching out her fork as if she were stretching her arms, she allowed the utensil to fall on the cover with a loud clatter. The noise startled Aunt Catherine awake with a jerk.

"As I was saying," she declared quite loudly to Mr. Worthy, "Georgiana is an accomplished player of the pianoforte. She will oblige us with some music after dinner."

"How wonderful!" Lord Robert chimed in. He had been speaking with Mr. Bennet on his other side but now took fresh interest in their discourse.

Georgiana was not fond of being ordered around, but she was accustomed to her aunt's imperious ways, and anything was an improvement over a lecture on fertilizer. She seized on the change in subject. "Are you very fond of music?" she asked Mr. Worthy.

"Music?" He stared into space with an abstracted expression as if she had given him an exotic fruit to taste. "Music...hmm...I am not sure...." He frowned. "I suppose...in small doses."

Georgiana and Richard exchanged a glance; his expression was so comical that she had to stifle a laugh behind her napkin.

"I love music," Lord Robert declared decisively. "I am particularly fond of Mozart."

Georgiana smiled to thank him for the rescue. "Yes, Mozart is one of my favorite composers."

Mr. Worthy cleared his throat loudly as if piqued that her attention had focused on another man. "I like Mozart, too."

Oh, merciful heavens! The man was impossible. "And what think you about art?" Georgiana asked Mr. Worthy, curious about what response he might give.

He frowned. "Art can get quite messy, particularly painting. I suppose drawing is not quite so troublesome."

Georgiana coughed to cover her laugh. Richard's eyes danced with merriment. The man who spoke at length about fertilizer thought *art* was excessively messy?

"Georgiana is accomplished at drawing," Aunt Catherine intoned.

Mr. Worthy seemed unsure what to do with this piece of information, but the viscount exclaimed, "Indeed? I must see some of your drawings."

Georgiana felt her face heat. "Sir, you are too kind."

"I am sure they are magnificent," he said sturdily.

"How could you possibly know?" Mr. Worthy asked peevishly. "You have not seen her artwork!" Clearly Mr. Worthy did not understand the rules of empty flattery.

Even Aunt Catherine was miffed. "Georgiana's skills are quite advanced, I assure you. And her playing..."

Lovely. Now her aunt spoke of her as if convincing bidders to buy a cow—albeit a very talented cow. Aunt Catherine could continue in this vein all night. Georgiana cast about for some kind of distraction. When her aunt paused for breath, Georgiana took the opportunity.

"Sir," she addressed Mr. Worthy, "did you know that Rosings Park has experienced a blight upon its potatoes?" The man's eyes widened in alarm while Aunt Catherine gaped. "And I believe they have not rotated crops in their wheat fields for years!" Finally, a benefit for enduring

William's many conversations with their aunt about modernizing her agricultural techniques.

"B-but, that is n-not—!" Aunt Catherine spluttered.

It was far too late. Mr. Worthy had grasped the subject like a dog with a bone.

He turned his full attention on Aunt Catherine. "Tell me the appearance of the blight. Spare no detail!"

On her ladyship's far side, Lord Robert smiled conspiratorially, recognizing Georgiana's maneuvering. But before she could engage him in conversation, Mr. Bennet said something to him, and they were soon deep in discourse.

Georgiana was not unhappy. In fact, she was quite relieved. She finally had an opportunity to speak with Richard without interruption. He was grinning at her. "Cousin, remind me to never fight you in a duel. You show no mercy."

She surveyed the table, but no one paid them the least heed. "She brought the man to Pemberley." Georgiana gave him her best innocent expression. "She should not be denied the benefit of his expertise."

Richard nodded in solemn agreement. "'Tis only fair."

Georgiana smoothed the napkin in her lap. "While you are here, we will have a match, will we not?"

"Of course. You merely need name the time and the place."

"Not tomorrow, but perhaps the day after—if the weather continues fine." Richard and William were the only ones who would shoot against her. Most men would be scandalized if they knew she could wield a pistol. "I have been practicing," she warned him.

"So have I," he said. His smile reminded her that he practiced his target shooting in exotic locations such as Spain and Portugal. Georgiana had no desire to go to war, of course, but it would be exciting to visit other lands.

"Tell me stories of the war," she asked him. "William always believes it will disturb me. And the newspapers have too few details."

"It is not suitable conversation for a young lady."

Georgiana rolled her eyes. "I promise not to faint." Still, he hesitated. Finally, she placed her hand on his where it rested on the table. He startled at the touch of her skin but did not withdraw his hand. "I pray *you* do not treat me as spun glass. I am not as delicate as everyone believes."

"I know, dearest." He held her eyes, and something taut inside her chest relaxed, like a bow being unstrung. He did know she was not the fragile flower everyone else appeared to see.

Finally, he blew out a breath. "I will tell you some of what I know—what I am allowed to tell civilians. But you must do something for me in exchange."

"Something for you?" She gave him a mischievous glance. "Would you like me to tell you what I know of the latest fashions in London? Or perhaps the most recent gossip in the *ton*?"

He held up his hands in surrender. "Spare me! No. I would only ask that one day when it is just the two of us you play my favorite piece for me."

She treasured those moments when they were alone together. This was a very easy promise to keep. "Of course. I will always play for you, Richard."

***

At the opposite end of the table, Elizabeth was experiencing the onset of a particular headache she acquired only when her mother and Lydia were in the same room. Her mother did not seem to think it necessary to pause in her discourse in order to chew her food while Lydia was determined to enjoy as much of Pemberley's food as possible during the course of her visit.

Mr. Wickham had just explained that he would be removing to the Lambton Inn the next day.

"And why should that be?" Elizabeth's mother inquired as she applied herself to her plate. "You know, Lizzy, these beans are a little undercooked. You should speak to your kitchen staff."

Elizabeth blinked. "I quite like them."

Mrs. Bennet shook her head. "Terribly bland." The last of the beans disappeared from her plate and into her mouth.

Lydia heaped more beans onto her plate. "I agree, Mama. Quite bland."

Mrs. Bennet focused again on Mr. Wickham. "So why must you be removed from our company?"

He granted her his most ingratiating smile. "It is Mr. Darcy's request, madam," he said smoothly with a little shrug that suggested he did not understand William's reasoning.

"I do not see why we should be deprived of your company," Mrs. Bennet said through a mouthful of beef. "It is most irregular."

Her husband tried to intervene. "Now, Fanny—"

She ignored him, her gaze shifting to Elizabeth. "Why would William be so high-handed?"

Elizabeth gritted her teeth and reminded herself that her mother did not know the full story of Mr. Wickham's deceit with Georgiana. Keeping her eyes fixed on her plate, she concentrated on maintaining a low, even tone. "William thought it was best for all concerned."

Mrs. Bennet flipped open her fan and vigorously fanned herself. "But it is a terrible thing that my youngest daughter should be ripped from my bosom!" *Oh, heavens,* Elizabeth thought. *Next she will be demanding her vinaigrette.*

Mr. Bennet patted his wife's hand, apparently hoping to calm her down. "I daresay we can bear the deprivation."

Lydia cut into her second helping of beef. "I shan't be ripped from your bosom. I will stay here at Pemberley—with you and Papa."

She will? Upon reflection, however, Elizabeth was not surprised that Lydia preferred the comforts of Pemberley. *How much more beef must Cook buy now?*

Mrs. Bennet was hardly mollified as she chewed ferociously at a piece of meat. "But what if the French should come to Derbyshire?" she cried. "Who shall protect us if Mr. Wickham is not with us? He is a soldier in the regulars." She turned to Elizabeth. "Lizzy, this beef is hardly tender. I must speak with your staff about how we cook beef in Hertfordshire."

Before Elizabeth could reply, Lydia laughed. "Mama, the French shan't come here."

Her mother nodded frantically as she cut more meat. "They will invade soon! Why, the very thought of it has quite demolished my appetite. Mr. Wickham must rally the footmen to the defense of Pemberley." The image of liveried footmen defending Pemberley from an invading horde of French soldiers threatened to provoke Elizabeth's laughter, but she clung to her composure.

"Fanny, we are too far north for the French," Mr. Bennet said firmly, but she waved his objection away.

Elizabeth leaned forward to pat her mother's hand. "Colonel Fitzwilliam shall protect us, Mama. He has been fighting Napoleon for many years."

As she finished her last piece of beef, Mrs. Bennet cast her eye dubiously down the table at William's cousin. "But he is so terribly old! How can he lead the men to victory? No, we must keep Mr. Wickham here!"

Elizabeth would not trust Mr. Wickham to defend them against a four-year-old boy with a stick. "The colonel is not old, Mama. He is five and twenty."

Her mother waved away this objection with a piece of bread. "You must speak with your husband about this immediately! I will not rest easy unless Mr. Wickham is here to keep us safe from the French marauders."

By now her shrill words had attracted the attention of the diners at the head of the table, who stared with expressions ranging from disbelief to horror.

Elizabeth looked imploringly at her father, who gave a quick nod. He placed a bottle in front of his wife. "My dear, you simply must try this excellent claret."

Elizabeth frowned. Her mother had an excessive fondness for claret, but it had a soporific effect on her. He poured into his wife's glass directly from a wine bottle. *Where had he obtained an actual bottle rather than a decanter—in which the claret would be diluted?*

Mrs. Bennet took several gulps until her glass was empty. "That *is* rather good. Quite a bit better than the other wine." She indicated a decanter as her husband refilled her glass. "You should speak with your butler. The state of the wine cellar could be improved," she told Elizabeth. Her mother quickly emptied her glass.

From the other end of the table, William raised a quizzical eyebrow at Elizabeth. She simply shrugged. She would not interfere with her father's strategy. Hopefully her mother would doze off before she said anything truly mortifying.

"Mark my words, Lizzy." Her mother's words were slowing noticeably. "The French will come any day. You must prepare Pemberley!"

"I will speak with William about it," Elizabeth promised, although she did not plan to advocate any actions.

"Good." Mrs. Bennet drained her last glass. Then her head fell abruptly down onto the table, and she began to snore.

Apparently not noticing, Lydia took another bite of a roll and asked, "Mama, when do you think the French will attack?" When her mother did not respond, Lydia grabbed her arm and shook her. "Mama? Mama?" Only a scowl from her father forced her to desist.

Elizabeth could feel her face heating and fought a sudden impulse to hide under the table. Everyone was staring at her mother and Lydia, including the viscount and Lady Catherine. *Why, oh, why could I not have been an orphan?*

Only William's eyes were on Elizabeth; she wanted to shrink away from his gaze. She had embarrassed her husband in front of his family— in his own house. Where was a hole to crawl into when she needed one?

When they had wed she had promised herself that he would never regret it, yet here she was mortifying him after less than six months of marriage. Still worse, how could she avoid such future embarrassment? Aside from barring her family from Pemberley, how could she have prevented the present situation?

Her father was unsuccessful at waking his wife enough to take her upstairs. Elizabeth gestured for two footman to help him; they regarded her parents disdainfully as they helped her mother to her feet. Even the staff thought she had brought disgrace to Pemberley.

She thought longingly of her quiet, warm bedchamber where no eyes would watch her. But she was the lady of the house and had no choice about her actions. She rang the little silver bell by her plate. "I believe it is time for the sweets course."

Chapter Three

The next morning Richard guided his horse along the path through Pemberley's woods. Although the trees had lost their leaves, they still had a kind of stark beauty silhouetted against the pale winter sky. Heavy clouds overhead threatened rain for later in the day. He always enjoyed snow during the yuletide season, but Richard appreciated the unseasonably warm weather they had been experiencing. The bite in the air was enough to clear his head without making him long for a warm hearth.

Tell me stories of the war.

When he closed his eyes, Richard could recall the husky tones of her low alto, the tilt of her head, the sparkle in her eyes. Everything about her was enchanting.

Months ago when he started experiencing such feelings for his cousin, he had attempted to forget them, to deny them. However, they were just as unforgettable as Georgiana herself. Whenever his thoughts were not completely devoted to some other subject, his mind would dwell on her—whether he was in her presence or far away on some war-related mission.

At first he had attempted to suppress such thoughts; she was officially his ward after all, although all of the actual raising of Georgiana had been left to Darcy. They had played together when she was small, but he had been in the army for most of her formative years. With a relationship built upon infrequent visits home and sparse correspondence, he had been more of a guardian in name than in fact—although Darcy had kept him apprised of her milestones. Upon his return from the Peninsula in February, Richard discovered Georgiana had blossomed into a beautiful young woman who was forming independent ideas about her life and had little desire for guidance from anyone.

Richard had found this more mature Georgiana very appealing but had fought any romantic fantasies. Ultimately he had conceded defeat, deciding such thoughts did no harm if he confined them to his own mind and never acted on them.

At dinner she had been uncommonly lovely, wearing a blue gown that complemented her eyes and coloring perfectly. Richard indulged in a fantasy of touching the golden curls that had shone gently in the candlelight. Would they be as soft and silky as they looked?

He chuckled again as he recalled how she had neatly turned the difficult Mr. Worthy on their aunt! It was brilliant. Georgiana was quite clever and surprisingly stubborn at times; it was a shame she did not have more confidence in her own judgment.

Fortunately, Georgiana would not allow herself to be pushed into marrying a man as insipid as Mr. Worthy. However, the viscount was a different story. The reins dug into Richard's hands as he clenched them tightly. Lord Robert was quite an eligible match, with a good income and noble lineage—and an estate which would allow Georgiana to live near Pemberley. He appeared to be perfect for Georgiana in every way.

Richard hated him.

He ground his teeth. *She sought* me *out for conversation and entertainment,* he reminded himself. But he knew that any such reassurance was false. She must wed eventually. If it was not the viscount, it would be another man. Indeed, Lord Robert was surely only the first in a long string of men who would seek Georgiana's hand. Her dowry was one of the best in England. Men whose family fortunes were suffering would want her to shore up their finances while the wealthy men would see it as a coup to win such an heiress.

Next year Georgiana would come out and officially be part of the marriage market. A familiar dread clawed at Richard's chest. *This is how it must be,* he reminded himself for the thousandth time. *I must bow to the inevitable.* However, this repetition did little to ease his heart.

The thought of her coming out made his heart race and his palms sweat. What if unworthy men preyed upon her? What if she fell for a scoundrel? Although she could not be his, Richard wanted to be by her side as she navigated the treacherous waters of the *ton.* But in all likelihood he would be on the Peninsula when she came out—and it provoked a unique sense of helplessness.

Richard shook his head to dispel the gloomy thoughts. The chances were good that all would be well. She would find a wealthy landowner or some duke's son with whom she would be very happy. And she would never know the truth in Richard's heart.

Richard reined in his horse. He had arrived at the turn in the path where he must proceed on foot. He tied the horse to a tree branch and forged his way through the undergrowth, following the faint signs of a long-overgrown path. Despite all attempts to silence his footsteps, he could not help breaking the occasional twig underfoot or rustling the leaves of a bush as he passed. With any luck, however, there would be no ears around to hear.

He neared the lightning-struck tree at the edge of the small pond where he and William had enjoyed swimming as boys. The low tones of a mourning dove sounded from nearby. Cupping his hand over his mouth, Richard returned the signal. The other man quickly materialized so smoothly out of the woods that he might have been part of the foliage. "Colonel." The man nodded his head in greeting. "A fine day for an outing." His French accent was quite evident.

"DuBois." Richard removed his riding glove to shake the man's hand. "Are you sure you were not followed?"

"*Non.*" The man raised an eyebrow at Richard. "Are you sure nobody suspects *you*?"

"Everyone believes I am simply visiting family for yuletide," Richard replied.

"Very good," DuBois responded. "So we may proceed with our business."

***

Darcy straightened his cravat as he strode toward Pemberley. Wickham was safely stowed at the Lambton Inn, and Darcy had rented the room for a week. Hopefully the Wickhams would be gone by then. *At least that resolves one of my headaches.* Unfortunately, the number of remaining headaches was sufficient to keep him occupied for the rest of the day.

Why must Elizabeth and I possess such troublesome relatives? Darcy wondered as he neared Pemberley's grand front entrance. Or perhaps the better question was: why were the troublesome relatives the ones who visited? Why could it not have been Charles and Jane who showed up unexpectedly on their doorstep? Or some other reasonable relative like…? Darcy thought for a moment. As Georgiana and Richard were already at Pemberley, he could think of no other candidates.

The moment Darcy pushed open the solid oak front door, his ears were assaulted by a piercing shriek. "Oh, Mr. Bennet! You have no compassion for my poor nerves!"

Elizabeth's father stalked down the staircase while his wife fluttered behind him. Elizabeth trailed after them, rolling her eyes. *Perhaps I should have stayed longer with Wickham*, Darcy mused—and then immediately recognized it as a sign of desperation.

The moment Mrs. Bennet saw Darcy, she hurried up to him. "Mr. Darcy! How fortuitous you are here! You must begin drilling your men immediately."

Darcy blinked. "My men?"

Behind Mrs. Bennet, Elizabeth had a hand covering her mouth. Was she trying not to laugh—or cry?

"This morning the maid told me that the footman had told her that his cousin had heard that the maid at the Lambton Inn said there was a Frenchman in town!" Mrs. Bennet announced triumphantly.

She paused to await his reaction.

"Indeed?" Darcy finally said.

"Yes! The Frenchman had lunch at the inn yesterday."

"I see."

"Do you not understand the import?" Mrs. Bennet asked. "He must be a scout!"

"Scout?" Darcy asked blankly.

"For the invading force!" Mrs. Bennet explained. At this pronouncement, Mr. Bennet threw his hands in the air and stalked out of the room.

Darcy massaged the back of his neck with one hand. "There are many French men and women who live in England. Most escaped from the ravages of the revolution and fled the guillotine."

She lowered her voice. "But why would such a person be in Derbyshire—so far from the coast?"

Elizabeth rubbed her temples as if a headache were coming on.

Darcy decided to take another tack. "Madam, the French army is quite occupied fighting in Spain right now. I am certain they have no intention of invading England."

"But the paper described *unusual* troop movements! And French ships have been spotted by people in Brighton and Dover!"

"*France* is not far from Brighton and Dover," Darcy pointed out. "So one might reasonably be expected to see French ships from there."

Elizabeth chimed in. "Even if France were to invade, we are very far north here. It would take them a long time to reach Derbyshire."

"That is what they want us to believe," Mrs. Bennet said in a tone so low it was practically a whisper. "They want to lull us into a sense of safety—and then they will attack!"

"We *are* safe," Darcy insisted. "We are very far from France here. I assure you—"

Mrs. Bennet interrupted him. "You must prepare to defend Pemberley! Your footmen must train every day. Are any of your tenants versed in weaponry?"

Darcy sighed, beginning to understand why Mr. Bennet's response to his wife's tirades was often silence. "I do not know. Although my steward might."

She gave an approving nod.

There must be some way to distract this woman! Surely she could not think about imminent invasion every minute of the day. "Have you been to visit the shops in Lambton?" he asked her. "Mrs. Reynolds said the milliner has just received some ostrich plumes."

"Ostrich plumes!" Mrs. Bennet's face lit up. While popular in London shops, the feathers were rare in the country.

"One of the footmen could escort you into town," Darcy offered eagerly.

She pursed her lips. "But they must stay and drill."

Of course.

"Papa can take you," Elizabeth volunteered. "It is the least he can do."

Perhaps there was a way to temporarily rid them of another troublesome guest. "Would Mrs. Wickham like to go as well?"

"An excellent suggestion!" Mrs. Bennet cried and ran for the bottom of the stairs. "Lydia! Lydia!" Her voice echoed and reverberated off the marble throughout the hall.

Darcy winced as Elizabeth gave him an apologetic look. While Mrs. Bennet made a commotion bellowing and ascending the steps, Darcy sidled over to Elizabeth. "Do you recall those ostrich plumes we bought for Georgiana that she did not care for?" Elizabeth nodded, understanding dawning in her expression. "Would you be so good as to ask Mrs. Reynolds to collect them and send them to the milliners immediately? I believe I can delay your parents' departure sufficiently."

Elizabeth's eyes sparkled with mischief as she set off in search of the housekeeper.

Chapter Four

Georgiana was weary of hiding in her bedchamber. After the tiresome conversation at dinner the night before, she had resolved to avoid Aunt Catherine, the viscount, Mr. Worthy, and, of course, Mr. Wickham. But keeping this resolution had required her to remain ensconced in her rooms for most of the morning.

She finally descended the stairs, hunting for companionship and eager to show someone her latest landscape drawings. Any friendly face would suffice. Perhaps Elizabeth or William or Mr. Bennet, who seemed kindly and of a good understanding.

But where was Richard? He had ridden out early, and she had expected him back before now. He always appreciated her drawings, pointing out features he particularly liked. And perhaps she could confide to him how uneasy she felt when confronted with two suitors.

Carrying her drawings, Georgiana ventured into the gallery, which was devoid of occupants. It was a long, narrow room, painted a vivid blue and lined with paintings of her ancestors on one side and a row of windows on the other.

Even when it was overcast like today, it was a pleasant room. She stared out the nearest window, watching the relentless drip-drip of rain onto the soggy lawn outside. It was not pouring, but surely it was enough to encourage Richard to return from his ride. *What if he is avoiding me? What if I annoy him with my immaturity?* Perhaps he did not believe that fleeing Rosings was the behavior of a mature adult.

William was a wonderful brother, but he was so concerned about her future that he never simply *listened* to her. Georgiana loved Elizabeth as well, but she was very caught up in her new life as mistress of Pemberley. Only Richard seemed to understand her fears about the future: coming out and choosing a husband—and her anxiety about disappointing everyone.

Or had he been indulging her? Did he still see her as a small girl he needed to watch over? Her chest tightened at the thought.

He never shows any signs of feeling more than friendship, she reminded herself. He listened attentively and sympathetically. But he dances with elegant women at balls and escorts them to the theatre. *I will never be like them.*

And yet a foolish part of Georgiana could not help hoping for something else. It was a silly, girlish fantasy that she must set aside. *I am a woman of marriageable age. I must be rational; there are plenty of other men who would gladly court me.*

A throat was cleared behind her. Could it be Richard?

Georgiana whirled around. Lord Robert and Mr. Worthy stood in the doorway, watching her avidly. Her feet itched to flee the room, but now was a good time to exercise her new resolve.

"Miss Darcy." Mr. Worthy gave a slight bow. "A lovely day, is it not?" Behind him, Lord Robert's lips twitched.

Georgiana glanced at the rain, which had grown heavier. "It would be lovelier with sunshine."

Mr. Worthy crossed the room, gesturing dramatically out the window. "Oh, do not say so! For the rain is most beneficial to the crops. Without rain no wheat would grow."

Georgiana blinked. "In December?"

On the other side of the room, the viscount appeared to examine the family portraits with great interest, but he did not hide his smile.

Mr. Worthy scratched his head, momentarily nonplussed. "Well, of course, there are no crops now, but the water falling now will help the wheat grow in the spring."

Georgiana could summon no response to this conversational sally; her interest in crops had already been exhausted. She gazed out the window once more. "Most artists prefer to draw sunny days, but I enjoy drawing landscapes in the rain. It changes the quality of the light and intensifies the colors."

He frowned as if she spoke a foreign language. "Rain is beneficial," he insisted as though precipitation could not be artistic and beneficial at the same time.

"Indeed," she agreed blandly, glancing sidelong at the viscount, who was still perusing the paintings. Surely he would rescue her from this conversation soon!

"My estate comprises nearly three hundred acres," Mr. Worthy remarked suddenly.

How could she respond to such a non sequitur? Georgiana pictured what Mrs. Annesley would say.

"How nice for you," she said finally. Of course, Pemberley was more than eight hundred acres.

Nodding his head absently, Mr. Worthy stared at the wet lawn outside the window. "I wonder how much rain has fallen."

"There is a rain gauge in the garden," Georgiana said.

The man's whole face lit up. "Indeed?"

"Yes, the head gardener can show it to you. Mr. Giles would know where he is."

"I *have* been meaning to discuss fertilizer with the gardener!" Mr. Worthy rubbed his hands together in eager anticipation. "If you would excuse me." He gave her a little half bow and strolled out of the room.

Lord Robert watched the other man leave and then gave Georgiana a small smile. "I hope you are not offended that Mr. Worthy finds rainfall totals more interesting than conversation with you."

"Not at all!" Georgiana laughed. "My companion, Mrs. Annesley, says there is someone for everyone. So perhaps there is a woman somewhere who finds rainfall totals and fertilizer to be the language of love."

He gave her a broader smile. "She would be a most singular young lady." His eyes sought hers; they were quite a vivid blue. "But I do not believe such discourse is the way to *your* heart."

As her face heated, Georgiana dropped her gaze to her shoes. Was it quite proper that he was discussing how to reach her heart?

The viscount appeared to be quite at ease, however. He indicated the landscapes clutched in her hand. "Are those some of your drawings?"

Georgiana had forgotten them. "Y-yes."

"May I?" Gently extracting them from her grasp, he held them up to the light to examine them. "Oh, these are quite delightful, Miss Darcy. I particularly like the way you dappled the light in this one…and the texture in the tree. Quite well done." He laid the drawings on a nearby table.

Of course he sought to flatter her; it was all part of the courtship dance, and yet his compliments still warmed her heart. "I do not give praise lightly," he insisted, tilting his head to meet her eyes.

"I thank you," she murmured, keeping her gaze downcast.

"So modest. I find it quite enchanting." From the sound of his voice Georgiana knew he had moved closer.

Should I step away? Is this proper? Do I even want him to be closer? Courtship was so confusing!

Unexpectedly, Lord Robert caught her hand, pulling her closer. She opened her mouth to object, but he pointed upward.

Oh, heavens! They were standing under a kissing bough, complete with oranges, ribbons, and mistletoe.

"I believe I may claim a kiss." Before Georgiana could protest, he pressed his lips against hers. She determined to allow the kiss; it would tell her more about this puzzling man. Yet she was unsure about the kiss itself. *Is it pleasant or unpleasant? Should I want more from him or pull away? Should I be feeling something different, or is this all there is?*

The act of kissing was perplexing. Georgiana could never know if she was supposed to want it or not. She was supposed to be demure and maidenly, but if she was expected to always avoid kisses, why was the tradition to hang mistletoe everywhere?

Mr. Wickham had kissed Georgiana exactly three times when he convinced her that he was in love with her. Those kisses had been pleasant, although the memory had soured when she recognized his insincerity.

The viscount's kiss, however, did not seem to share the passion of Mr. Wickham's kisses. *But what do I know of passion?* Mr. Wickham's passion had ever been false. However, Lord Robert's kiss was quite nice—and ultimately unobjectionable.

Finally, the viscount released her with a gentle smile. "I pray you forgive my presumption," he begged. "You presented such a pretty picture silhouetted against the window that I could not help myself." He reached up to pluck a berry from the mistletoe with a mischievous smile.

Now that the kiss was finished, she was still unsure how she felt about it. She found it equally difficult to settle on how she felt about the man. She only stared at him, breathing hard and wishing she could find her voice.

"Miss Darcy?" He regarded her with a furrowed brow.

"Lord Robert, I just recalled that I must help Elizabeth with something. I pray you excuse me." Before he could reply, Georgiana turned on her heel and strode from the room.

***

Richard had just gratefully given his wet hat and greatcoat into the care of a footman. *If only I had such help when I was campaigning!* That thought—and all others—fled when Georgiana strode into the marble hall. The expression on her face was odd, revealing nothing of her thoughts.

"Richard!" Her face lit up with a brief smile as she walked toward him. "I wondered where you were. Did you get very wet?"

He grinned at her. "Moderately so, but I believe I will survive."

She reached out for an unexpected but welcome embrace. Richard gladly enfolded her in his arms, as she rested her head on his chest. "Is something amiss, dear heart?" he asked.

Georgiana pulled far enough away to look up at him. "Not really. Life is confusing sometimes."

He chuckled softly. "That it is."

Catching some movement from the corner of his eye, Richard turned his head to find the viscount entering the hall from the gallery—the same door Georgiana had used. Had he been with her alone? Richard stifled a pang of fear and anger. She would tell him if the man had disturbed her, would she not?

Lord Robert crossed the hall on his way to the stairs, his steps echoing off the marble floor. His mouth tightened as he noticed Richard and Georgiana holding hands; he nodded a greeting to Richard but did not stop. Georgiana darted a quick look in the man's direction and then turned back to Richard. "Will you listen to me play my new piece? I am a little anxious about it."

He gave her hand a squeeze. "Of course."

Georgiana's pace was brisk as they walked to the music room, but a subtle stiffness in her shoulders suggested tension. Richard managed to hold his tongue as they walked, but it was a battle.

They achieved the room, and Richard closed the door softly behind them. "Georgie? Were you alone with Lord Robert?"

She hesitated a moment, holding herself very still. "Yes," she finally replied. In the ensuing silence she seated herself on a settee near the door.

Richard was proud that he did not immediately start to curse and throw things. "Did he hurt you? Disturb you?"

She slowly shook her head. "No. He-he…um…kissed me."

The words shocked him like he had been struck by lightning. "Kissed you?" He was practically yelling.

"Under the mistletoe in the gallery." Her tone was so matter-of-fact that Richard could not discern her sentiments.

He swallowed back his anger. "Did you wish him to kiss you?" he asked.

"I…I…did not object." She frowned.

The words drained the energy from Richard's anger. He sank onto the settee next to Georgiana.

She continued, staring at nothing in particular. "I wanted to see how his kiss would compare."

"Compare?" Richard asked.

"To Mr. Wickham's," she clarified.

Damnation! Richard's hands clenched into fists. He should be grateful that Wickham had gone no farther in compromising Georgiana, but the thought of the blackguard's hands on her...his lips on hers...always provoked the desire to strangle the man.

She tilted her head, considering. "The viscount's kiss was quite...pleasant."

Pleasant? Richard hated the man for having a pleasant kiss. *But then if she kissed me, she would be describing it as a damn sight better than pleasant!* No. That was an unworthy thought. *We shall never kiss like that.*

"Forgive me for saying so, darling," Richard said, "but you do not act like a lady who had a pleasant experience."

"I am not sure I should have allowed it. But Lord Robert does seem like a very pleasant man."

Pleasant again. No one was likely to ever describe me in such terms. Thank God.

But what if she wants a pleasant man? Someone who does not lead a life of excessive excitement—including battles and death? Someone whose passions did not run too deep? What if that was her ideal man? Richard suddenly felt quite cold.

If that is what she wants, I cannot stand in the way of her happiness. He could deny her nothing, not even this. "Do you like him?" Richard forced the words out.

She hesitated for a moment. "I do. He is amusing and kind. I would like to know him better."

Richard's insides had turned to ice. *Breathe in. Breathe out. She has not agreed to a courtship or engagement. She has merely expressed an interest.* He nodded, meeting her eyes with an effort of will. "He will be at Pemberley quite a while. You will have many opportunities to converse."

"Yes. How fortunate." Georgiana did not smile; rather she seemed a bit troubled.

However, Richard could not bring himself to continue the subject. "Now, I would like to hear you play. Perhaps the Mozart piece?" he asked.

Georgiana smiled as she stood and made her way to the instrument.

Chapter Five

Mrs. Reynolds seemed to be not quite herself today. The housekeeper had been an invaluable resource when Elizabeth had become the new mistress of Pemberley; she kept the house humming efficiently. Every morning the housekeeper met Elizabeth in her sitting room to review the household plans for the day. But today Mrs. Reynolds was distracted and a little gloomy, which did nothing to assuage Elizabeth's already troubled mood. Her family was creating endless sources of vexation, and their presence was wearing on William after only two days.

Elizabeth tucked her feet under her on the settee and scrutinized the supper menu once more. "Perhaps some marmalade to go with the ham tonight?"

When Mrs. Reynolds did not respond, Elizabeth looked up. The housekeeper shifted uncomfortably in her chair. "I know it is a little old-fashioned to serve it with dinner rather than breakfast, but Mr. Darcy does like it with his ham," Elizabeth added.

Now the housekeeper looked even more uneasy. "That's not it, ma'am. It's…well…we have no more marmalade. Cook has sent to Matlock for it, but it will not arrive today."

"No more marmalade," Elizabeth repeated. Such a thing had never happened in all her time at Pemberley. The house always seem so well supplied and well prepared for any eventuality. "Why is that?"

Mrs. Reynolds' hands twisted in her lap. "To tell you the truth, ma'am, it was all consumed…"

Elizabeth frowned. Yes, they had been hosting many guests, but the staff usually kept a plentiful supply of the preserves on hand. *Who could have—? Oh!* "Mrs. Wickham ate it?" Lydia had always over-indulged in the treat.

The housekeeper nodded.

Still, that was a lot of marmalade. "How much breakfast could she possibly—?"

"Begging your pardon, ma'am, but it isn't just for breakfast. Between meals she has asked for something to tide her over. Tea on trays in her room—and the like."

"How often?"

Mrs. Reynolds swallowed. "Three times yesterday."

Elizabeth sat back in her chair, realizing she should have anticipated this. Lydia no doubt viewed a visit to Pemberley as an opportunity to indulge in the kind of lifestyle she felt she deserved but could not afford. "What else has she requested?" She gritted her teeth, afraid to hear the answer.

Mrs. Reynolds hesitated.

"Please tell me the truth," Elizabeth said. "I will not think less of you."

The housekeeper nodded, taking a deep breath. "She has had Jenny remake her muslin gown. Maggie mended another gown and fixed two of her slippers. She drank a bottle of one of our oldest wines in her room alone. She wished to ride Miss Georgiana's mare, but the stable boy would not saddle her. When Mr. Lafitte was here to paint Miss Georgiana's portrait, she asked him if he would do a miniature of her, but he did not have time." She finished with a sigh and an apologetic look at Elizabeth.

Lydia had only been at Pemberley two days! Elizabeth massaged her forehead. This must cease before William discovered how Lydia was taking advantage of their hospitality. It would only confirm his low opinion of her family.

"Very well. If my sister has any more…unusual requests, please come to me before you grant them. She is not the Queen."

A grin flitted over the housekeeper's face. "Yes, ma'am."

"And that is true for my mother and other guests as well," Elizabeth added.

"Our biggest trouble with Mrs. Bennet has been supplying her with a sufficient quantity of smelling salts."

Elizabeth rolled her eyes. "And the other guests? Are they presenting problems?"

Mrs. Reynolds shuffled the papers in her lap, studiously looking at them. Elizabeth waited. "Nobody except Lady Catherine," the older woman finally confessed. Elizabeth raised an eyebrow in silent inquiry. "She was unhappy with the curtains in her room."

Elizabeth's eyebrows shot up. "The curtains?"

"She claimed they allowed in too much light, and they had a musty odor." Mrs. Reynolds pursed her lips. "I assure you we clean them very frequently."

"Of course. You keep an exemplary household." The woman looked faintly relieved. "How did you resolve the problem?"

"Two of the footmen removed her curtains, and we switched them with the curtains from the rose bedroom."

Elizabeth rolled her eyes. *What a terrible bother.* "You have the patience of a saint. Is there anything else I should know?"

Mrs. Reynolds hesitated and then spoke. "Lady Catherine said she cannot digest mutton. So we will need to serve beef while she is here."

"Very well." Elizabeth pressed her lips closed to prevent errant thoughts from escaping. "Is there anything else?"

"Yes, Lady Catherine also cannot abide peas, leeks, carrots, cow's milk, Stilton cheese, white wine, and plum pudding."

"Plum pudding!" Elizabeth cried. "We cannot have yuletide without plum pudding."

Mrs. Reynolds' brows knitted together. "Perhaps Cook can find an alternative."

"Perhaps Lady Catherine can do without dessert," Elizabeth said tartly. "I am sorry the unanticipated guests have caused so much extra work for you and the staff."

"I hired some extra help from the village, so we are not faring too badly. Although Jenny was in tears yesterday after Lady Catherine yelled at her because the bath water was too warm. Jenny is not accustomed to…well, Mr. Darcy never yells."

Elizabeth was indignant. The Pemberley servants did an excellent job, and the family rarely had cause for complaint. They did not deserve such treatment from a guest. *Perhaps I should ask William about it. But I do not want him to think I cannot manage a few guests. And would he be pleased if I bring him a complaint about his aunt?* "If such a thing occurs again, I pray you inform me so I may intervene," Elizabeth told Mrs. Reynolds.

"Thank you, Mrs. Darcy." The older woman smiled as she stood.

Elizabeth shook her head. "Lady Catherine derives no pleasure from visiting Pemberley; it seems to be nothing more than an endless source for complaint. I wonder why she stays. She arrived on the slimmest pretense, and her visit has no purpose." Mrs. Reynolds' eyebrows rose, but she stared fixedly at the door. "Do you know something I do not?" Elizabeth asked.

The other woman did not respond immediately. "It would do me a service if you help me navigate this situation," Elizabeth prompted.

The housekeeper continued to stare into space. "I do not want to speak out of turn, ma'am. But this has happened before—Lady Catherine comes for a long visit, demands the best treatment, and will not leave."

At least my presence did not provoke such behavior.

The older woman spoke almost as if the words were being drawn from her. "Mr. Darcy mentioned to me…she is very…frugal with her household expenses and does not keep her manor fully staffed. But she likes a little luxury: eating beef and hot baths every day."

"She visits so Pemberley will bear those expenses rather than incurring them at Rosings Park," Elizabeth realized. "That is…diabolical. Why has Mr. Darcy not taken her to task for it?"

Mrs. Reynolds shrugged. "He wishes to keep the peace within the family. She has also grown more…particular with each visit. The curtains have never offended her before."

Now Elizabeth understood the situation more clearly, but there was no easy way to resolve it. She and the Pemberley staff must cater to Lady Catherine—likely until Twelfth Night.

She nodded to the housekeeper. "I pray you do inform me if there are any other difficulties." *Although what can I possibly do? I am the last person Lady Catherine will listen to.*

Mrs. Reynolds reached out for the doorknob. "I will, ma'am."

"And," Elizabeth added before the women left the room, "please do not trouble Mr. Darcy with *any* of these details." Mrs. Reynolds regarded her quizzically. "He is weighed down by enough concerns." *And he need not know the full extent of my family's demands on the household.*

"Very well." Mrs. Reynolds nodded but looked uncertain as she exited. Elizabeth stared at the sitting room's striped wallpaper for a long moment. Her father had promised they would be gone by Twelfth Night, and the other guests would also leave by then in all likelihood. But it seemed very far away at this moment.

***

William had issued dinner invitations to Mr. Peters, the local curate, and his wife, Lord and Lady Pippinworth, and the dowager viscountess Lady Agatha, Lord Robert's mother. Perhaps he had believed that the presence of strangers would encourage family members to be on their best behavior. If so, Elizabeth thought, he was sadly mistaken.

Lady Catherine complained loudly to Lady Agatha about the shades of Pemberley being polluted. Mr. Worthy completely occupied Georgiana's attention with a discussion of manure output, apparently under the mistaken impression that such a subject was a part of traditional courtship rituals. Meanwhile, the viscount glared at Mr. Worthy but was too well-bred to interrupt. Lydia consumed everything on her plate, belched loudly, and then brashly asked for more. Whenever her wineglass was in danger of running dry, she demanded that the footmen refill it. Elizabeth's mother was having a quiet conversation with Mrs. Peters, but Elizabeth could hardly hope such civility would last.

Lady Catherine examined her wine glass. "There is a spot on my glass," she announced loudly during a pause in the conversation. "I require another one." A footman rushed to take it from her. She addressed Elizabeth despite having more than half a table between them. "Your staff has overcooked the roast. I will need to speak with them about it."

"I thought it was delicious," Richard said stoutly.

"How kind of you to take an interest," Elizabeth said to her mother without glancing up from the meat she was cutting.

Mrs. Bennet's vivid portrayals of a French invasion were, unfortunately, beginning to whip Mrs. Peters into a frenzy. After a particularly lurid portrayal of streets running with blood, the poor woman grabbed her husband's arm. "Did you hear, John? Perhaps we should remove to my parents' house in Newcastle." She turned quickly to Mrs. Bennet. "Do you suppose we will be safe there?" Elizabeth's mother blinked, not sufficiently versed in English geography to offer an opinion.

"Mrs. Peters," William intoned, "I do not believe there is any cause for alarm."

"But would it not be prudent to ensure our safety?" She addressed William, but her eyes implored her husband.

Mr. Peters gently disengaged his wife's hand from his arm. "I cannot flee to Newcastle, darling. I must remain here and tend to my flock."

"But I cannot leave you here!" she cried, drawing the eyes of everyone at the table. "I could not bear the thought of you spitted at the end of a French bayonet—or blown into pieces by a cannonball."

Suddenly not quite so hungry, Elizabeth set down her fork.

Elizabeth's mother patted Mrs. Peters' hand. "There, there, my dear. He is a clergyman. Certainly the French would not kill him." The woman's shoulders sagged with relief as Mrs. Bennet continued. "At most they would put him in a lice- and rat-infested prison." Mrs. Peters' face took on a greenish tinge.

Both William and Georgiana also laid down their forks. Lady Pippinworth took a hasty sip of wine. At this rate no one would finish their meal except Elizabeth's mother…and Lydia.

"Mrs. Bennet," William said. "I hardly—"

"This beef is tremendous!" Lydia declared to no one in particular. "I would like some more." All the eyes at the table turned toward her.

"It is ham," her father, seated next her, whispered loudly.

Lydia frowned and peered at her plate where only a few shreds of meat remained. "Hmm…I thought the taste of the beef was a bit off." She turned around in her seat, presenting the rest of the table with her back, and addressed the footman behind her. "Are you certain it is ham?"

The man did his best not to laugh. "Yes, ma'am."

"Well, I would like some more." Lydia turned back toward the other diners, producing a little giggle for no discernible reason. In the middle of the table, Lord and Lady Pippinworth talked to each other in hushed tones; Elizabeth could only imagine what they were saying.

"And when fed the right kind of hay, each cow can produce up to sixty-five pounds of high-quality manure a day!" Mr. Worthy's voice broke through the sudden silence. "Can you imagine? Sixty-five pounds!"

Mr. Peters and Mr. Bennet set down their forks almost simultaneously. Georgiana, to whom this remark was addressed, covered her mouth with her napkin, but the crinkles around her eyes suggested that she was suppressing a smile.

At the end of the table, William took a very deep breath and closed his eyes. He opened his eyes and continued in a deliberate, reasonable tone. "Perhaps we could—"

His words were eclipsed by his aunt's voice. "In its acute phase, Anne's illness requires that she be bled at least one or two times a day," she explained to Lady Agatha. "The doctor prefers to use leeches. He is rather old-fashioned."

The footman had offered the platter of ham to an enthusiastic Lydia and then Elizabeth's mother, but all of the other diners appeared faintly nauseous. Georgiana's complexion was quite pale while William's face had turned red. Mrs. Peters' hand covered her mouth. Lord Pippinworth eyed the clock as if wondering when he could politely depart.

Surely there was some means of diverting the dinner party's attention from this utter disaster. But when Elizabeth saw William's red, stricken face, all innocuous subjects of conversation fled her mind.

Elizabeth had long grown accustomed to the embarrassment her family heaped upon her, but she imagined William's eyes held the dawning horror of a man who understood precisely what kind of a family he had attached himself to.

Colonel Fitzwilliam cleared his throat. "Georgiana, I believe you are learning a new piece on the pianoforte?" Elizabeth wanted to hug William's cousin.

Georgiana seized on the topic of conversation with alacrity. "Indeed! It is a piece by Bach. Quite difficult but hauntingly beautiful."

"Is it ready to perform?" Elizabeth's father was not a great music aficionado; he must have been as desperate as Elizabeth for a new topic of conversation.

"Not quite yet," Georgiana replied. "But I can play something else this evening if you would like."

"Georgiana is quite proficient," Lady Catherine declared. "But the instrument here is not as fine as the one at Rosings Park." She looked pointedly at Elizabeth. "You may not recognize a truly high-quality pianoforte, but I can recommend the man who provided mine."

Elizabeth regarded the woman coolly. "Actually the pianoforte is quite new. William purchased it recently for Georgiana's birthday."

"It is quite good for my purposes," Georgiana said stoutly. "I like it."

Lady Catherine gave her a withering look. "You should hold higher standards."

Colonel Fitzwilliam rubbed his hands together briskly. "Well, I am hoping for some Christmas songs this evening." He turned to Georgiana. "Would you play some? I always enjoy such music during the yule season."

"Oh, of course," Georgiana responded.

The conversation continued along this innocuous vein for some time, allowing Elizabeth to breathe more easily. But she did not dare glance at William for fear of what she might see in his face.

Chapter Six

Darcy was relieved to gain the sanctuary of his bedchamber. While the men had drunk port and smoked cigars after dinner, Worthy and the viscount had vied subtly to demonstrate how each would be the best candidate for Georgiana's hand. Worthy was an impossibility. She would be far better remaining a spinster than marrying that buffoon. If Georgiana informed Darcy that she wanted to marry Worthy...well, first he would need to ascertain that she had not been at the sherry.

Lord Robert was another matter altogether. There was nothing objectionable about the man, save that he was a bit forward in advancing his own cause. Georgiana did not seem to dislike him, although she showed no sign of any particular regard.

Darcy constantly reminded himself that she was of a marriageable age. Based on the expression on Richard's face when he regarded Lord Robert, Richard was experiencing similar difficulties. Only a few years ago, it seemed she was climbing trees and running footraces. Now she was a young lady. Indeed, she had requested to delay her coming out for a year, and Darcy had not objected. Next season she would be a year older than the other women coming out for the first time.

Darcy shrugged out of his coat and untied his cravat. Unfortunately, Aunt Catherine seemed to believe there was a great hurry to see Georgiana wed. When the gentlemen had joined the ladies after dinner, his aunt had again expounded the virtues of her chosen candidates. Apparently she hoped to have some influence over the affairs of Pemberley if Georgiana married one of her relations.

Darcy rubbed the back of his neck where a headache was forming. The dinner had been a farce in every possible way. He could not invite anyone else to Pemberley until all of their guests had departed. Which meant that their yuletide season would be full of belching women, strident complaints about the food, and lurid tales of French invasion. It had only been a day since he had sent Mrs. Bennet and Mrs. Wickham to shop, but he might need to subsidize another trip on the morrow.

And then the discourse about bloodletting and manure... *I am master of Pemberley, and yet I cannot even ensure civil conversation at my own dining table!* As he unbuttoned his waistcoat, Darcy mused how he had always prided himself on cordial relationships with family members. Even as others allowed petty squabbles to impair the bonds of blood, Darcy had managed to place family loyalty above such trifling concerns. Tonight, however, he had come perilously close to venting his frustrations. *It will not do! I must find a way to regain my equilibrium.*

The door adjoining the sitting room clicked open, and Elizabeth, dressed in her night clothes, slipped into his bedchamber. He stiffened. How could he prevent his foul mood from affecting her? He did not want to risk the possibility that he might speak of his irritation—particularly when her family formed part of his frustration.

"William?" He must have appeared quite forbidding, for her brow was creased with worry. Obviously he was not fit for human company.

He sighed. "Dearest, I feel a headache coming on. Perhaps it was too much port. I think I would better rest alone tonight."

She assumed a rather fixed smile. "Of course. Is there aught I can do? Would you like a massage?"

Heavens, that would be lovely. But could he avoid the temptation to speak ill of her family? He sank down on his luxuriously appointed bed, rubbing his forehead. "No, I thank you. I will retire for the night."

Her feet turned toward the doorway, but still her eyes remained on him. They had spent every night together since their wedding, except for the few days when she had taken ill in September.

"Perhaps we should discuss the guests and our plans for tomorrow?" For some reason the hesitation in her voice annoyed Darcy. "We could—"

Darcy waved dismissively. "I spent all day with our guests. I do not need to discuss them as well." The words emerged more sharply than he intended, but he was too weary to even think about them. Why could she not understand that?

Elizabeth nodded, biting her lower lip. "Of course. I will bid you good night."

"Good night." At the sound of the door closing, guilt flooded Darcy's veins. But the headache was now pounding in his temples, demanding that he sleep.

I should talk with her…explain…in the morning, he thought, right before he closed his eyes.

***

Elizabeth crossed the sitting room between their bedchambers, feeling a bit like she was not there at all. Everything felt so unreal. Her head had become disconnected from her body, which still automatically negotiated the way to her room.

I will not cry. Do not think about his words, she admonished herself. *Focus on something else.* Her eyes picked out a Chinoiserie vase against the far wall. *Why had the potter chosen those colors? Had he noticed that small imperfection near the lip of the vase?*

Within seconds she was through the door and into her own bedchamber. *The fire is low. I must ask Mary to put an extra log on it tomorrow night.* Elizabeth climbed into her bed. A small tear in the coverlet caught her attention. *I will have Jenny mend that tomorrow.*

The pressure behind her eyes built, threatening tears. *What if William thought—? No. I must think about something else or...*

Once the tears started flowing, Elizabeth knew it would be difficult—if not impossible—to check them. Opening her eyes, she sought a source of distraction. The flickering light from the fireplace cast distorted shadows on the bed's canopy.

When she and Jane had trouble sleeping as children, they would label those shadows and giggle about them. This one was a dragon. That one looked like Hill when she bent over. The next was a gnarled tree. *Oh, if only I could have Jane with me now!*

But her sister was not here, and Elizabeth was mistress of Pemberley, for better or worse. She blinked suddenly moist eyes and forced her focus on the dancing shadows. *That one looked like a tiger on the prowl...the next a rather pointy flower...*

***

The next morning was little better. Customarily, Elizabeth enjoyed the company of others and would spend hours discussing books and other subjects with their many guests. Today, however, every time she closed her eyes she saw her lonely bedchamber swathed in shadows. The memory followed her around like a ghost dedicated to haunting her.

Her foul mood was evident to others. Jenny had gaped after Elizabeth said a harsh word to her. And Lydia had sighed loudly and rolled her eyes at breakfast when her sister was less than patient.

She needed a refuge where she could be undisturbed for an hour or more. As Elizabeth strode through the corridors, she considered her options. The music room. She and Georgiana had begun the task of assembling boxes as gifts for the servants and some of the needier tenants for the day after Christmas. But the boxes were far from finished. Indeed, filling boxes, tying ribbons, writing tags—that would occupy her restless mind.

When Elizabeth opened the door, her eyes fell on the boxes and piles of clothing and other gifts. *Oh dear, there is quite a bit of work to be done!* Only then did she notice that the merry notes of "Good King Wenceslas" on the pianoforte had faltered to a stop. *Oh! I must be truly oblivious not to have noticed Georgiana practicing.*

"I am sorry! I will return another time." Elizabeth immediately retreated from the doorway.

"No! Stay, Sister!" Georgiana jumped up from the piano bench. "We...should finish assembling the boxes."

Elizabeth stepped into the room, closing the door behind her. "I must confess those were my thoughts as well, but if you want to practice..."

Georgiana slipped out from behind the pianoforte and seated herself at the work table, piled high with boxes and gifts. "No. I-I would prefer to talk, if you do not mind."

Sensing that her sister-in-law had something particular to discuss, Elizabeth took another chair. They were silent for a few minutes. As Elizabeth folded a long scarf, she asked, "Were we to give this to Bolton or Williams?"

"Bolton," Georgiana said decisively.

Elizabeth placed it into the appropriate box.

Georgiana sorted pairs of gloves. "How many children live with Widow Graves?"

"She has three," Elizabeth responded. "And we should give her a pair as well." Georgiana put four pairs of gloves in one of the boxes.

Elizabeth kept her eyes focused on her task lest she make Georgiana self-conscious, but finally she decided to broach the subject. "Did you wish to discuss anything in particular?"

Her sister-in-law chewed on her lower lip. "How can you tell when...you like someone?" Elizabeth frowned, not understanding the question. "I mean...a...man? If he likes you. How do you know if you like him?"

Ah. This must be about Lord Robert. Elizabeth nearly smiled at the earnest anxiety on Georgiana's face. "If you like a man well enough to consider marrying him?" she asked, and the other woman nodded. "Well, I am of the opinion that one should not marry without love—the very deepest love. Although not everyone believes that."

"But how can you know if you are in love?" Georgiana's eyes fixed on the ribbon she tied around one of the boxes, but her entire attention was on the conversation.

"I am certain it is different for each individual. But when I fell in love with William"—she could not help smiling at the memories—"I thought about him all the time. I wanted to be constantly in his presence. He made me laugh. I was always happy to be around him."

As Elizabeth spoke, Georgiana's mouth dropped open slowly. "Oh...*oh!*"

Was Georgiana realizing she had feelings for the viscount? It would be a brilliant match. Lady Catherine would be pleased, and it would help to mend the relations between their families. William would be pleased as long as he was convinced Georgiana would be happy. "Is that how you feel?" Elizabeth asked, adding some sweets to one of the boxes.

Georgiana's eyes slid away from Elizabeth's. "P-perhaps...I...do not know..."

"If you think you are in love with someone," she said carefully, "and he is a man of good character, you should...explore the possibility." Georgiana had not known the viscount long, so it would behoove her to learn more about his character.

Georgiana considered this for a moment. "However, there are...difficulties. I do not know how he feels about me...."

Elizabeth pursed her lips, considering her answer. *How did you recognize love? How could you trust that love?* "If a man truly loves you, then he will be willing to accept you as you are—without seeking to change you."

Georgiana's faraway look suggested that she was pondering Elizabeth's words, but her brow was still deeply furrowed. Elizabeth wanted to embrace her and chase the apprehension away.

"There is no need to rush. I am sure Lord Robert will be willing—"

Georgiana's head jerked up suddenly. "Oh! It is not Lord Robert."

Surprise temporarily deprived Elizabeth of her words. "Mr. Worthy?" Elizabeth finally croaked out.

"Heaven forbid!" Georgiana laughed. "I cannot muster enough enthusiasm for agriculture."

In the ensuing silence, Georgiana did not volunteer a name. Who else could it be? Since she was not yet out, Georgiana's circle of acquaintances was necessarily small, and her exposure to unmarried men was very limited. *If I demand to know his identity, will that prevent her from confiding in me in the future?*

Biting her lower lip, Georgiana finished tying a ribbon around another parcel and added it to the stack. Then she squeezed Elizabeth's hand gently. "Thank you, Sister. You have given me much to think about." Without another word, she rose and slipped from the room.

Elizabeth stared after her. Who was the man Georgiana might be in love with? What if it was someone unsuitable? A servant? What possible advice could Elizabeth offer then?

And what would William think when he found out?

Chapter Seven

Richard was not surprised that Darcy wanted to ride, nor that he asked his cousin to accompany him. He *was* surprised, however, at the alacrity with which Darcy enacted the plans once Richard had agreed. By the time Richard had changed into riding clothes, Darcy was already out at the stables. And by the time Richard had his horse saddled and mounted, Darcy had already started on the path.

When Richard caught up to Darcy, he slowed his horse from a trot to a walk. "You are riding as if the hounds of hell are at your heels," Richard joked.

Darcy grimaced. "Not the hounds, but perhaps the relatives from hell."

Richard nodded. The houseful of relatives at Pemberley was a minor annoyance to him, but it must be a major thorn in Darcy's side. "That particular group of people can be…trying."

Darcy snorted at this understatement.

They rode in silence for a few minutes. Darcy's eyes were fixed on the path before them. "Elizabeth and I were planning a quiet yuletide season, just the two of us. The autumn was very busy and—I believe—difficult for her as she learned the ways of being mistress of Pemberley."

Was this a hint? "Oh, damn, Darcy. I did not know. Would you like me to leave?"

Darcy shook his head vigorously, and Richard released a relieved breath. "I pray you do not. You help make their company more bearable."

"I wish there were more I could do."

Darcy quirked an eyebrow. "If you could arrange to have Wickham press-ganged into the navy, that would be most helpful—and I pray you take Worthy while you are at it."

Richard laughed. "If only I could. I long to slay *all* of Georgiana's dragons." Then he caught his breath. *Have I revealed too much?*

But Darcy did not take any particular notice. "I am of two minds whether I should also wish away Lord Robert."

"But he is a lord!" Richard exclaimed.

Darcy shot him a look. "Do you think I care aught for that?"

Richard's hands moved restlessly on the reins. "There are few men in England whose fortunes would equal Georgiana's—men you could be sure were not merely seeking her dowry."

"For that reason, she is likely to marry a man who has less."
Richard scrutinized his friend's face. *Did that disturb Darcy?* "But that
means nothing if the man will make Georgiana happy."

Does he really believe that? "It does not bother you?" Richard
asked.

"No. As long as I am convinced the man loves and cherishes her."

"But disparities in fortune—"

Darcy interrupted with a sharp shake of his head. "I was once
overly concerned about issues of fortune and social standing. It nearly
cost me my greatest happiness. I am fortunate that Elizabeth forgave my
arrogance." He shot Richard a sidelong glance. "I would never let such
considerations stand in the way of Georgiana's happiness."

They rode in silence as Richard considered Darcy's words. *Can I
trust them? Am I making the same mistake as Darcy, placing too much
emphasis on rank and fortune?* Perhaps they were not so great a barrier as
he supposed. Difficult relatives notwithstanding, Darcy was deliriously
happy with Elizabeth.

But there were other obstacles. "Do you think Georgiana is much
taken with Lord Robert?" Richard heard himself ask his cousin, although
he instantly wondered if it was a good idea.

Darcy did not immediately reply. "I do not know," he said finally.
"He is a pleasant fellow from a respectable family. There is no reason to
dislike him."

This was not exactly a hearty endorsement, but Richard would have
expected caution from Darcy on this question.

"What think you of the man?" Darcy asked.

How can I answer the question? I am hardly impartial. "I agree.
He is quite pleasant," Richard finally said, ignoring any pangs of jealousy.

Darcy shrugged. "Ultimately it is Georgiana's decision. We can
only hope to guide her on the right path."

"Indeed." However, Richard doubted his ability to guide her in any
objective way.

"And what about you, Fitzwilliam?" Darcy asked. "I have not
heard any recent tales of your adventures. Have you encountered any
likely ladies?"

Richard kept his eyes on his horse's neck, attempting to banish any
visions of Georgiana's smile or her golden curls. "No. I find it more and
more difficult that any women will meet my standards." *Except for one.*

"Well, do not let it go too long, or all the eligible ladies will be taken. You are already of an age."

"Yes, as Mama reminds me constantly," Richard said with chagrin.

Darcy laughed. "Being married is a wonderful state. I heartily recommend it." Richard felt another twist of jealousy but for a different reason. Although he did not begrudge his cousin any bit of happiness, he could not help wishing he could experience such bliss. However, it was unlikely to come Richard's way. "Perhaps Elizabeth could introduce you to some of the local ladies," Darcy said.

The thought of courting a woman who was not Georgiana made him nauseous. "No!" he said immediately. Darcy's eyebrows shot up, and Richard immediately modulated his tone. "Do not go to any trouble on my account. I may never marry. I am a second son after all."

Darcy frowned, prepared to object, but Richard forestalled him. "Do you think it looks like rain? Perhaps we should turn back."

***

When Georgiana left the music room, her head was full of Elizabeth's words. Paying only the scantest attention to her surroundings, she ran right into Mr. Worthy, who promptly dropped a jar he was carrying. Fortunately, the jar did not break, but it spilled its contents all over the floor.

"My seed wheat!" Mr. Worthy exclaimed, his eyes wide with horror.

"My apologies!" Georgiana immediately knelt to help him clean up the mess.

They both gathered handfuls of wheat to pour back into the jar. As they scooped and dumped the grain, Mr. Worthy explained, "This is quite a rare strain which Pemberley's steward gave me." His lips twisted peevishly. "I hope it is not contaminated."

"If it is, I am certain Mr. Markham will give you more," Georgiana said. "I am sorry."

He nodded jerkily. "You should be more careful where you walk."

Georgiana's shoulders tightened. It was easy to see where his priorities lay. Did he believe this was an effective way to woo a woman?

The last bits of wheat were in the jar. Georgiana brushed off her hands and wondered when she could wash them. Mr. Worthy scrutinized the jar to discern how much wheat had been lost. "Well, I suppose it is not too much of a disaster," he admitted.

"I am glad to hear it, Mr.—" Georgiana began, poised to continue down the corridor.

But he took her by the arm. "I have not had the opportunity to tell you why this wheat is so special."

Georgiana's determination to be polite could not compete with the sense of dread that gripped her heart. "I am afraid I am in a bit of a hurry—"

"No matter. Look." He pointed upward with a sly smile.

Georgiana had a sinking feeling that she knew what she would see. Of course, a kissing bough hung from the ceiling. Why had Mrs. Reynolds felt compelled to hang them all over the house? Mr. Worthy reached up to pluck a mistletoe berry. *Oh, I cannot wait until all the berries are gone!*

His grin made her feel like he were running his hands over her body, and she shuddered involuntarily. *And I thought nothing would be worse than discussing fertilizer!*

He leaned toward her. "Of course, I must claim a kiss."

***

As Richard and William neared the stables, they discovered Georgiana dressed for riding. A groom was saddling her mare, Athena, a spirited beast who danced and twitched under the groom's hands. Georgiana was scarcely less agitated; she shifted from foot to foot and tapped her fingers restlessly against her thigh. "Are you off for a ride, Georgie?" Darcy asked her.

"Yes. I feel the need for some exercise." She pulled on her glove with a sharp, quick movement as she said to the groom, "Not the sidesaddle, Billy. The other one, if you please."

The groom nodded, removing the sidesaddle and hefting a standard saddle onto the horse. Only then did Richard notice that Georgiana wore one of her specially made dresses with a split skirt.

Richard lifted an eyebrow. More than once Aunt Catherine had lectured Georgiana on how a proper young lady should only ride sidesaddle. Of course, her ladyship believed Darcy had been lax in allowing his sister to ride astride when she was younger. Recently, Georgiana had been making an effort to abide by their aunt's dictum, but apparently today she was not in a conciliatory mood.

Darcy opened his mouth as if to remind his sister of their aunt's words. She glared at him with a lifted chin and flashing eyes. He closed his mouth again. *Clever man.*

Georgiana tugged irritably on one of the saddle's straps with quick jerks.

"Is something amiss, dearest?" As Darcy climbed down from his horse, his eyes stayed fixed on his sister.

"No. Nothing." She bit off the words.

Darcy and Richard exchanged raised eyebrows behind her back. *Perhaps Georgiana should not ride alone.* Richard inclined his head in her direction. "Would you like some company on your ride, or are you determined to rid yourself of all human contact?"

She glanced up at him, blue eyes fringed with long blond lashes. Richard's heart started beating faster. She shrugged. "You may accompany me if you wish."

"It would be my pleasure."

One side of Darcy's mouth quirked up. "I thought you were concerned about rain."

"All the more reason to go," Richard asserted. "She should not be…alone in the rain…by herself should it come to that."

Darcy was baffled, unsurprisingly; Georgiana had certainly ridden solo in the rain many times.

"I will not melt," Georgiana muttered. Without the assistance of the groom, she swung herself into the saddle.

Richard nudged his horse closer to hers and leaned forward to murmur in her ear, "To own the truth, I am just as happy not to return to the house yet. It is a bit crowded."

She frowned. "I do not disagree. At this point I would be happy to never return." She wheeled her horse around and urged it into a canter once they had cleared the stable. Richard exchanged another concerned glance with Darcy before turning his horse to follow her.

Once on the road, Georgiana urged her horse to a gallop; Richard kept pace. He was all for a bracing ride, but what was the reason for Georgiana's mood? *Well, I must be prepared to give her whatever she needs.*

Without warning, Georgiana urged her horse into a flat-out run, leaving Richard in the dust. Her mare was a thoroughbred, bred for speed. While Richard's horse was fast, he had been chosen more for his stamina and steadiness in battle. Richard ceased any attempt to catch Georgiana and settled into a fast trot, reminding himself that she was a very accomplished rider and unlikely to fall from her horse.

Georgiana was very far ahead of him when she finally slowed her mare to a trot and then a walk. As he drew level with her, however, her expression was still stormy.

The path wended around a large pond that the cousins had dubbed "Mirror Lake," a favorite swimming and fishing destination when they were children. As they drew close, Georgiana reined in her mare and slid to the ground, tying her horse's reins to a tree. Richard followed suit, accompanying her to the shore of the pond.

She stared disconsolately at the pond for several long minutes. "Do you wish to discuss what is troubling you?" he finally asked in a low voice.

Heedless of her clothing, Georgiana perched herself on a large moss-covered rock. "No, but perhaps I should."

Richard nodded encouragingly but said nothing, waiting for her to decide when the moment was right. For a long time she remained silent, but then she sighed. "What would happen if I did not have a coming out?"

Richard's eyebrows shot up. "You mean you do not want to do it next year?" With a coming out planned for the following year, Georgiana would already be a year older than most of the other women taking their bow. If she delayed it further, she would be quite a bit older, no doubt raising some eyebrows.

Georgiana picked up a leaf and shredded it in her fingers. "I mean that I do not want to come out at all."

"But girls love their debuts! They dream about it."

Georgiana frowned ferociously and leaned forward, throwing her arms around her knees and drawing them close to her body. "Not every girl," she ground out.

"But, surely—"

"Take care that you do not start sounding like your mother," Georgiana said acidly.

Richard bit back a hasty retort. Perhaps his response had been…unconsidered. If there was one thing he knew about Georgiana, it was that she was not like other women. "You are correct," he said quickly. "It may not be to everyone's taste."

"And yet everyone needs to suffer through it!" The words practically burst out of Georgiana as she shot to her feet. "Why should I have a coming out when I have no desire for it?" She paced. "Everyone will know that I am of age." She gave a harsh laugh. "Clearly Lord Robert and Mr. Worthy do."

Richard blinked. He had never considered whether women needed to come out and endure all of the related fuss. He very much enjoyed balls and other society in town, but it would be a strain for someone more retiring like his fair cousin. Even Darcy hated the circuit of *ton* events, and he was more sociable than his sister.

Georgiana was still speaking, striding back and forth along the narrow strip of grass by the pond. Richard had never witnessed her talk so rapidly. "I already hate this!" She gestured emphatically in the direction of the house. "Men vying for my attention, complimenting me, begging to escort me into dinner."

"Most women would enjoy that."

Georgiana threw her hands in the air. "I suppose I am an aberration then."

Richard wanted to bang his head on the rock. He had done it again. "No! I did not mean—" He paused to collect his thoughts. It was essential that he consider his responses with Georgiana, not recite the standard lines. Then another thought occurred to him. "Did something happen, sweetling?" *If one of the men had treated her inappropriately, God help him…*

"Mr. Worthy kissed me," she said through clenched teeth. "Under the mistletoe."

Damn mistletoe! What a stupid tradition anyway. Richard grappled with his jealousy—apparently she had hated the experience—but that still left anger…. "I will speak with him and ensure he treats you more appropriately," Richard volunteered.

She shook her head. "I have no difficulty telling him that his attentions are unwanted." She bit her lip. "It is not that. It is…" Her voice trailed off, and Richard waited while she gathered her thoughts. "Mr. Worthy and Lord Robert…all day they tell me how pretty I am…how accomplished…how special…"

Richard furrowed his brow. "But you are—"

"It does not matter what I am!" she cried, gesticulating wildly. "Do you not understand? They would say it no matter what. Not because it is true, but because they want my hand—and my fortune. I could have three eyes and blue horns, and they would tell me I have a unique form of beauty or some such rot!"

Her vehemence made him blink. "Surely some of their compliments are sincere."

"Some!" she spat. "That is the dilemma. I do not know what I can believe—what I can trust!"

Oh. "Because Wickham told you the same things?"

She whirled away from him, staring at the pond. "Yes! And I believed him. And none of it was real!" She glanced over her shoulder with a hard, bitter smile. "He only wanted my fortune. Just like these men."

"So we should seek suitors who will insult you?" Richard asked with a smile.

She snorted a laugh. "No, but..." She brushed hair from her face. "How am I to trust anything they—or any of my suitors—say?"

"You will grow more discerning as you meet more men, have more experience."

"But I do not want more experience!" she growled. "I hate doing this dance with two men. How will it be with ten or fifteen or twenty?"

Unfortunately, Richard mused gloomily, those were not unreasonable estimates. *Damnation! If I thought it was painful watching two men ply her with compliments, how will I survive hordes of them?* Hopefully fighting the French would prove sufficiently distracting.

"You are a clever girl," he told her. "Have confidence in yourself and your judgment. No doubt you will navigate the waters of the *ton* very well. You will be the toast of London. Everyone will be clamoring to dance with 'the young lady from Derbyshire.'"

This only made her scowl again. "And how many will seek my favor if they know I am not a proper young lady?"

He hated to hear her disparage herself like that. "Of course you are! You—"

"No, I am not, Richard," she interrupted. "Even if you set aside my shameful history with Mr. Wickham. I like to ride astride. I shoot guns for pleasure. I have no interest in fashion. I would rather play the pianoforte for hours than converse with a gentleman. And I *loathe* London!"

Hmm. Georgiana's tastes had always been a bit...unconventional. Richard had always assumed that she would settle into more ladylike pursuits as she matured. But why was that required? Surely she could remain herself and still find a husband.

Still, his stomach clenched. Perhaps those goals were incompatible. Aunt Catherine's answer was to change Georgiana, but Richard did not care much for that solution. He liked her as she was—and presumably Georgiana did as well. Richard would hate to give up riding astride and shooting; why would it be different for Georgie? But could she find a husband who would appreciate her unique qualities and allow them to flourish?

"I am sure most gentlemen will be understanding—"

Georgiana snorted. "Mr. Worthy was alarmed to find that I enjoy shooting pistols. And Aunt Catherine already warned me against mentioning to Lord Robert that I ride astride."

Yes, both gentlemen would be eager for a wife who conformed more closely to acceptable ladylike behavior. "If they are not right for you, I am sure that somewhere there is a man who would find it acceptable—"

"Acceptable, but not appreciate it," she remarked acidly. "I do not want a husband who would 'tolerate' my greatest enjoyments in life, and I do not understand why I need to go through the miserable process of coming out and having a London season to find this mythical creature. If he exists, he might not reside in London at all."

Richard opened his mouth to reassure her that such a man did exist but then closed it again. Besides himself and Darcy, he could only think of a few examples of men that tolerant—and they were married.

"I do not want to come out. I want to live in Derbyshire and do the things I love." She seemed to shrink in on herself as she stared wistfully down at her hands.

"I understand," he said immediately.

"Do you?" Her eyes searched his.

He took both of her hands in his. "Yes. But, dearest, what if the right man for you lives in Sussex, and you can only meet him by going to London? You should not deprive yourself of the chance to meet your soul mate and fall in love."

She scowled so that all of her features scrunched up. "I shall not fall in love. Not ever!"

Richard would not have expected such vehemence from the normally gentle Georgiana. "But surely—"

"No." Her hands were balled into fists, and she scowled ferociously.

Recognizing a closed subject, Richard nodded. But his heart was sore. Wickham had so deeply scarred Georgiana that she believed she was incapable of love. That such a beautiful, gentle creature should think that of herself…Richard wanted to weep.

He pulled her into his arms, holding her closely in a way he had not allowed himself recently. She relaxed against him. She was tall—he liked that—and could press her face into his shoulder while he stroked her back soothingly. *You already have my love*, he told her silently. "No one will expect you to come out if you do not wish to, dearest," he said aloud.

"That would make me much happier," she murmured.

"I will speak with William," he promised.

"Thank you." Her words were muffled against his shoulder.

Finally, Richard compelled himself to release her and stepped away. "I wish for your happiness above all," he murmured. *If only she knew how true that was.* The worried lines in her face had softened. Perhaps he had restored a measure of peace to her. "You are my favorite cousin, of course," he said with a jaunty grin. Her tentative smile faltered, but he was unsure why. "Are you tired, dearest? Should we return to the house?"

She mustered a tiny grin and glanced up at the sky. "Certainly. It looks like rain."

Chapter Eight

"Mr. Wickham is here to see you, sir." Giles's tone suggested that a slug had demanded entrance. A disreputable slug.

Darcy bit back a groan. It was possible there were words in the English language he would find less welcome, but he would be hard-pressed to name them. *Damn the man!* Darcy was paying for his lodgings and had made it clear that he was unwelcome at Pemberley. What more could the man want?

At least Georgiana was still out riding with Richard; with any luck Wickham would be gone by the time she returned. Darcy had sent Mrs. Bennet and Mrs. Wickham shopping again, so there was relative quiet in the house. *And now Wickham comes to ruin it.*

I must simply be more forceful with the man. Darcy sighed. "Very well, show him in."

Within a minute Wickham sauntered through the door, his lazy smirk in place. Darcy wanted to smack it off his face. *Good Lord! How could I think such violent thoughts? Wickham is a bad influence even on me.*

Wickham gave Darcy a nod. "Good to see you, *Brother.*" The appellation was calculated to irritate Darcy. *And damn his eyes, it is working.* Wickham threw himself into the chair opposite Darcy's desk without awaiting an invitation.

Darcy glared. "I have already explained you are unwelcome at Pemberley."

Wickham put a dramatic hand to his chest. "Your own family! You wound me!" When Darcy carefully did not react, Wickham shrugged. "I thought you were unlikely to visit me in Lambton, and what I have to say is best not committed to paper."

Darcy felt a frisson of anxiety. Wickham's words were not likely to be good for the Darcy family. "Speak your piece and get out."

"Such lack of brotherly sentiment from someone who has known me all my life. I find it most upsetting." Wickham gave a mock pout.

Darcy kept his face stony.

Finally, Wickham straightened up and assumed a more serious tone. "The... business opportunity I mentioned before did not...bear fruit. I have need of additional funds."

Darcy's teeth ground together as he imagined what kind of "business" Wickham was conducting. "I already paid your debts to that blackguard in Lambton, and I am supplying your wife with more than pin money here. I believe that is sufficient."

Wickham coughed. "Unfortunately, it is not enough. I need more."

"If you are living beyond your means, that is not my concern," Darcy said stiffly.

Wickham's smirk turned into a broad grin. "That is where you are wrong, Brother." He leaned back into his chair, staring lazily at his fingernails. "Georgiana must be planning her coming out—and I have heard she is being courted by some eligible gentlemen."

Darcy hated hearing her name on that man's lips. "That is not your concern."

Wickham regarded him under heavily lidded eyes. "But it is. Imagine the scandal if the *ton* knew I had taken her maidenhead."

Darcy was on his feet and looming over his desk without any conscious decision. "You did not!" he shouted.

One side of Wickham's mouth curved up in a smile. "No, I did not. I should have when I had the chance. More's the pity." He shrugged carelessly; Darcy wanted to strike the man for that expression alone.

Perhaps he could wipe away Wickham's smile with his fist.

"Here's the rub: nobody really knows what occurred between me and Georgiana except us. And we were alone together in Ramsgate quite a bit. Mrs. Younge and other witnesses can attest to that."

Darcy pounded his fist on the desk. "You would not dare! You would not dare spread such slander!"

Wickham spread his hands in a conciliatory gesture. "Of course I would not...as long as I get what I want."

Darcy was grinding his teeth to stumps. He hated to even ask the question, but he had no choice. "What do you want?"

Wickham's smile was wolfish. "Georgiana's dowry."

Darcy was speechless for a moment. *Of all of the brazen—* He had never expected Wickham to say something *that* outrageous. "I am not giving you her dowry!" he shouted.

Wickham shrugged, remaining irritatingly calm. "Why not? It will be worthless to you once my rumors spread. No well-born man would want her if doubts are cast on her purity. Who would take that chance?"

Darcy silently cursed the man. He was right. Georgiana could certainly find *someone* who would marry her under such circumstances, but many men of quality would never consider an alliance surrounded by doubt and mired in scandal. And then there was the anguish it would cause Georgiana. It would destroy her to have her greatest mistake made public in such a way.

"I will give you ten thousand," he conceded.

Wickham laughed, a noise that grated on Darcy's nerves. "No, I want the whole thirty thousand."

Darcy ran both hands through his hair. If he gave Wickham the money set aside for Georgiana's dowry, then a new dowry would need to come from the estate funds. He could do so, of course, but he could not afford a full thirty thousand without selling assets and causing hardships to the tenants of Pemberley. Damn the man! He had Darcy over a barrel, and he was enjoying it.

"You bastard," he growled at Wickham.

Smiling broadly, Wickham stood. "I will leave you to contemplate your decision. But I will return in a few days and expect an answer then."

When the door clicked closed behind him, Darcy sank into his chair. *Good Lord, what can I do?*

***

Elizabeth had hoped William's mood would improve during the day, but by dinner time it was worse. Far worse. She had never seen him in such a black mood. He exerted little effort to participate in the discussion at the dinner table and barely responded when asked a direct question. His bleakness affected many of the other guests, and conversation around the table was rather stilted.

Only Elizabeth's mother remained unaffected, babbling nonstop about ribbons and lace, although it was an improvement over the hand-wringing about an imminent invasion. Lydia said little, mostly because she could barely insert a word into her mother's monologue. Mr. Worthy also seemed oblivious as he chattered on about chicken manure until Lady Catherine finally put a stop to it with a concise: "Do change the subject, or I will feed *you* some chicken manure." He was remarkably silent afterwards—for a whole five minutes.

Throughout most of the meal, Georgiana stared at her plate. Lord Robert tried to catch her attention with some pleasantries, and they engaged in some desultory discourse. Richard, who could usually be relied upon to provide vivid conversation, spent an inordinate amount of time staring at Georgiana and glaring at the viscount, although Elizabeth could not fathom why.

As hostess, Elizabeth's role was to encourage the flow of discourse, but whenever she glimpsed William's somber mien, she had little heart for the task. William's bleakness seemed to drain away all of her energy. Consequently, once the subject of the unseasonably warm weather had been thoroughly addressed, she lacked new subjects for discussion.

He is unhappy with my family and wishes them gone. They are an embarrassment and cause no end of trouble. And now he regrets marrying me. She leaned down to wipe her mouth, surreptitiously wiping her eyes at the same time. She had always feared such regrets but had not expected them quite so quickly.

If only I could present him with an heir! Elizabeth had been hoping for happy news about a new life on the way, but this morning had dashed those hopes. *It has been six months. Why have I not quickened? If I could give him a child, at least I would be of some value to him and the estate. Instead I provide him with nothing but troublesome relatives!* William's sober gaze fell on her; was that censure in his eyes?

She quickly glanced away, focusing her attention on the conversation at the table. Her father was attempting to direct the flood of words about lace, much as one might pile sandbags to prevent a deluge. "Yes, my dear. It does sound like a very fine purchase indeed," he said to his wife. "What do you propose to do with so many yards of lace and ribbon? Shall you have a new dress made?"

Mrs. Bennet smiled and fluttered her hands. "I shall have a new dressing gown made. That would be very lovely! Of course, it barely signifies as we shall all be murdered in our beds by the French army—and it will hardly matter what I am wearing then!"

Mr. Bennet could not help covering his eyes and shaking his head. Lady Catherine laughed aloud. Even Georgiana hid a smile. Surely there must be another possible topic of conversation—something safe and innocuous. Georgiana's music? No, they had already discussed it. Kitty and Mary's health? That subject had also been covered. Perhaps Jane and Charles—

To Elizabeth's surprise, Lydia chimed in. "Well, *I* shall be prepared if the French soldiers attack Pemberley." She smiled coyly.

Richard raised an eyebrow. "In what way?"

She giggled. "George has purchased me a pistol!" she squealed.

Oh, Good Lord, Lydia had a firearm? There were so many ways in which it was a bad idea that Elizabeth could scarcely count them.

Mr. Bennet's alarmed expression perfectly mirrored Elizabeth's sentiments. "Do you know how to shoot it?" he asked.

Before his daughter had an opportunity to reply, Mrs. Bennet felt the urge to issue her opinion. "Well, if the men of Pemberley cannot defend us, then perhaps the women will. I understand you also shoot, Miss Darcy?" Elizabeth cringed. She had once mentioned the fact to her mother but had never intended it as general dinner conversation. *I cannot expect discretion from Mama*, she concluded sadly.

Several pairs of eyes were fixed on Georgiana, who instantly turned pink. Lord Robert's face, in particular, was troubled by the information. Lydia, however, clapped with glee. "You have a pistol as well?" she asked Georgiana.

The other woman cleared her throat, staring at her plate. "Several, actually."

"She is an excellent shot," Richard said with a challenging look at Lady Catherine that dared her to object. "Better than I am."

Lydia's eyes grew wide. "Will you teach me to shoot at a target as well?" she asked Georgiana.

Georgiana bit her lip. "I have never given instruction before...but I suppose I could..."

This was a spectacularly bad idea. Elizabeth knew nothing good could come of it.

Lydia, however, bounced in her chair. "I will fetch my pistol, and you can show me the proper way to fire it."

Elizabeth opened her mouth to explain that dinner was not an appropriate time for target practice, but her sister was already halfway out of the door. She gave up that cause as lost and described plans for a sleigh ride if the weather cooled and they received sufficient snowfall.

A few minutes later, a loud bang sounded from upstairs, interrupting Mr. Worthy's disquisition on how snow affected corn blight. Richard rushed to his feet. "That was a gunshot!"

"It's the French!" Elizabeth's mother shrieked and dove under the table.

William stood so quickly that he overturned his chair. Both he and Richard rushed out of the door. They were back moments later with a red-faced Lydia. Black powder decorated the front of her dress, but she appeared unharmed. Elizabeth rushed to her sister's side.

"We encountered her on the stairs," William explained to Elizabeth.

"Are you well?" she asked her sister. Lydia giggled with the bashful air of a child who had been caught stealing biscuits. "La! I am unhurt!" She giggled again but then suddenly covered her mouth with her hand. "But, oh! I almost forgot. I may have set my bedchamber on fire a little bit."

Chapter Nine

An hour later, Darcy had beaten out the fire with the help of some footmen, and Lydia had been ensconced in another bedchamber. Darcy had appreciated but not heeded Richard's advice to lock her inside. Mrs. Reynolds and some maids were now dismantling the curtainss that Lydia had ignited. And after an hour of effort, Mr. Bennet had coaxed his wife out from under the dining table and taken her upstairs.

Aunt Catherine had decreed that they would play cards after dinner. But Darcy's foul mood meant he was unfit for human company; he had stalked down the hall to his study without learning if any others had agreed to cards.

He poured himself a brandy, wondering how much more trouble the Wickhams could inflict upon him in one day. At least burnt curtains could be replaced easily enough. What would he do about Wickham's threat?

A knock sounded at the door; it opened before Darcy even bade his visitor to enter. Richard slipped into the room and closed the door behind him.

Without a word, Darcy poured the man another brandy and handed it to him, then both men took seats by the fire. "You seem a bit out of sorts today, Cuz," Richard observed after taking a sip.

"Out of sorts? The girl set my house on fire!"

"Yes, she does have a talent for disaster." Richard waved this away. "However, I meant before that. You were dark and growly at dinner."

"Dark and growly?" Darcy raised an eyebrow.

Richard nodded. "Something else is bothering you."

Darcy examined the inch of amber liquid in his glass. He had contemplated telling Richard before; as one of Georgiana's guardians, his cousin had the right to know. However, the thought of seeking out the man and repeating Wickham's threats had made Darcy nauseous. Now Richard was here and asking about it…

Darcy leaned forward, his forearms on his knees. "Wickham was here today. He threatened to spread the news that…"—Darcy swallowed—"Georgiana is not…pure."

Richard shot to his feet and swore with a vehemence that Darcy had never heard before. "That bastard!" He called Wickham a parade of inventive names which reminded Darcy that his cousin did indeed serve in the army. Eventually he asked wearily, "What does he want?" Darcy hesitated. "With Wickham there is always a scheme," Richard observed. "What is it?"

Darcy sighed, hanging his head. "Her dowry."

"Damn the man!" Richard swung around and began pacing the length of the study. "You cannot give it to him!"

"I cannot allow him to spread rumors."

Richard froze in his tracks, eyes wide with horror. "They are false, are they not? He did not impose himself—?"

"No, nothing like that. He himself admitted that he never touched her." Richard visibly sagged with relief. "However," Darcy continued, "it would be all too easy to establish they were alone together at Ramsgate. Gossip would proceed from there."

"The blackguard! It could ruin her chances to marry."

Darcy set his glass down. "Even without the question of marriage…even if we could somehow convince everyone the story was untrue, the talk itself would destroy Georgiana."

Richard's eyes narrowed. "Perhaps not. Georgie is made of sterner stuff than I had suspected." Darcy wondered what could have occurred to give Richard that opinion. But then his cousin's pacing quickened. "Still, we cannot allow it to happen. I cannot wait until I get my hands on that scoundrel!"

Darcy stood quickly, blocking his cousin's path and placing a restraining hand on his shoulder. "Fighting with Wickham will not help Georgiana. It would only increase the odds that he would reveal what he knows."

"He cannot reveal it if I knock out all of his teeth!" Richard growled.

Darcy met his cousin eye to eye. "Richard, this is not helpful." The other man finally slumped under Darcy's hand, nodding wearily. "We must think of a strategy," Darcy continued.

"You cannot be thinking of acceding to Wickham's demands?"

"I hope it will not come to that…" Darcy said slowly. "I could not make up the difference without hardship to Pemberley, so she would be married with a lesser sum." He sank once more into his chair. "Of course, if she were married, it would be a moot point. Wickham would not dare to make such an accusation about a married woman, and the gossip would not travel far if he did. Do you think Georgiana likes Lord Robert?" he asked his cousin.

Why did he stiffen so? Did he dislike the viscount? After a long pause, Richard responded in measured tones. "I have not often observed them together. He seems like a pleasant young man."

"If she truly liked him, they could marry quickly, the viscount would get the dowry, and any words of Wickham's would be irrelevant. But I would not ask it of her unless she truly liked the man. Of course, she would not get a coming out…"

"I do not think that would trouble her," Richard murmured. "She told me today she is rather dreading her coming out."

Darcy raised his eyebrow at this information but then set it aside as a subject for another day.

"Marriage would be the easiest solution. Perhaps I should ask her about Lord Robert," Darcy said. "If he is not to be the one, then we will need to pursue other options."

Richard's expression was a little…odd. Pale and perspiring. Almost as if he did not feel well. "Are you all right, old fellow?" Darcy asked.

"Hmm?" Richard turned his head, but his eyes were unfocused, as if he did not really see Darcy or the room.

"Is there something the matter?" Darcy asked.

"No." He blinked. "I am well. Although perhaps I will speak with Georgiana, too."

"There is no need. I will ask her about Lord Robert," Darcy said.

Richard made a dismissive gesture. "Not about that. I must ask her something else."

And with that enigmatic statement, Richard strolled out of the study, leaving a frowning Darcy behind him.

***

Elizabeth pulled the covers up around her shoulders. Now she was warmer but no sleepier. She stared at the bed's canopy, willing herself to drowsiness. She had retired early for once, having depleted the energy required to manage her parents, sister, and other demanding houseguests—not to mention all of the staff who wanted her attention. Bed was her one refuge, the place nobody would disturb her, particularly if they believed she was asleep.

Her brain would not stop cataloguing the horrors of the past few days. Her mother threw everyone into a panic over a nonexistent and nonsensical invasion. Her sister was eating them out of the pantry. Her brother-in-law had forced William to pay for his stay at the Lambton Inn and reimburse his creditors. While Mr. Worthy and Lady Catherine were not Elizabeth's relatives, their presence certainly added to the household's strain. Georgiana was increasingly anxious around that particular "suitor," and Jenny had broken a teacup under Lady Catherine's critical eye.

And then Lydia had set fire to Pemberley.

Small wonder she was having a difficult time nodding off. Elizabeth covered her face with her hands as if she could shut out reality. She was not accustomed to this bed since she usually slept in William's room and only used this bedchamber to change her attire. The light was all wrong. The position of the fireplace. The hangings around the bed. Everything was askew.

She had considered seeking out William's bed for only the briefest moment. It was easy to imagine venturing into his room and experiencing another rejection. She grew even colder at the thought. He would not condemn her. No, it was worse; he would be disappointed. Elizabeth had brought her family and their troubles upon Pemberley—and she seemed singularly incapable of improving the situation even one iota.

She had tried to bring about changes. Her father had sympathized with her predicament but disavowed any influence over his wife's moods or whims. Her mother closed down any talk that even hinted at leaving the "security" of Pemberley. Lydia refused to remove to the Lambton Inn, giving a variety of paltry excuses. Mr. Worthy had proved immune to any of Elizabeth's gently worded hints that he might prefer the yuletide season at his own home. She had not yet attempted to dislodge Lady Catherine since that would likely cause more difficulties than it would solve. Unfortunately, that task would fall to William, should he even wish to attempt it. *Our first Christmas at Pemberley, and I cannot prevent our guests from transforming it into a farce.*

What must William think of her?

Elizabeth rolled to one side, closing her eyes tightly and resolving to think sleepy thoughts. But at luncheon that day her mother had related the story of Lucy Thomas, a woman from their neighborhood. A pretty woman, she had married very well, securing a wealthy landowner. But she had not produced an heir, and he had quickly tired of her. He sent her to a distant country estate while he inhabited their London townhouse with a mistress.

William would not do such a thing. He would never take a mistress. But if she proved too troublesome—and did not provide an heir—would he banish her to Pemberley or send her to another of his holdings? Her heart ached. *Of course he would not set me aside.* Yet in the deep recesses of her mind, a niggle of doubt remained.

They had planned for a quiet Christmas that would allow them to reaffirm their love; instead they were being driven further and further apart. Elizabeth's eyes burned, but she blinked fiercely to prevent the tears from falling.

The click of a lock alerted her that someone had entered the bedchamber. She closed her eyes and relaxed her features so as to appear limp and engulfed in dreams.

The firm, brisk footsteps were definitely William's. If only she could open her eyes and ask to be held—to demand his comfort. But she recalled his grim visage and terse responses from supper. What would she do if he refused or showed reluctance? Best not to even attempt it.

The footfalls arrived at the side of the bed, along with the soft sounds of his breathing. She kept her limbs relaxed, her eyes closed. What did he feel as he gazed upon her? Anger? Disappointment? Regret? Elizabeth only prevented a shudder of anxiety with an effort of will.

Finally, the footfalls retreated back to the door, and it closed behind him.

Only then did Elizabeth allow herself to cry.

***

I will not cry. I will not cry. Georgiana hurried down the corridor with her head bowed and all of her attention focused on reaching her bedchamber. She almost crashed into Richard.

"Whoa, Cuz!" he exclaimed. "Where are you rushing off to?"

Georgiana kept her gaze averted from his. Why must it be Richard? Few people could easily discern her feelings, but he was one. She quickly wiped away the angry tears with her handkerchief. "I must go to my room. I beg you to excuse me."

He caught her arm before she could rush past him. "Has someone upset you?" He craned his neck to meet her eyes.

"Please, Richard." She tried to pull her arm from his grasp.

"Who was it?" His tone was gentle but implacable.

She sighed. "Mr. Wickham." Richard swore under his breath.

"I was in the garden doing my target practice," Georgiana continued. "He came out of the house, claiming to seek Mrs. Wickham, but then said he wished to talk with me."

Richard's hand squeezed her arm. "About what?"

"I do not know." She swallowed. "I tried to stand my ground, but he kept coming closer and closer. I told him to stay away, but he kept walking toward me…and I did not want…" Her voice trailed off.

His gaze was intent on her. "You did not want what?"

"I did not want to shoot him. Although it was very tempting."

Richard broke out into peals of laughter.

Georgiana folded her arms across her chest. "Richard Fitzwilliam, it is not amusing! I was very angry. I could have seriously hurt him."

Richard wiped his eyes. "Aye, you could have. I am certain you would have done some damage."

She lifted her chin. "Murderous impulses are not ladylike."

"No, indeed," he agreed amiably, stroking his chin. "Mrs. Annesley would have been quite upset."

"I did not want to hurt him," she continued primly. "So I fled the garden. I know it is cowardly, but—"

"No!" he cried. "That was the best decision."

She gave him a half-hearted smile. "You should go to your room and ring for some tea," he said, glancing in the direction of the garden.

Georgiana had a premonition of disaster. "And where will you go?"

"I need to clear some things up with Wickham," he said grimly, striding toward the garden.

Georgiana hurried after him. "Is that a wise idea? Perhaps we should talk to William."

"Wickham and I will merely have a friendly exchange of ideas. I will ask him, for example, why he has the idea that he can visit Pemberley's garden when he has been forbidden."

Georgiana hurried to keep pace with him. "I do not want you to be hurt."

He gave a harsh laugh. "Oh, *I* will not be hurt."

"I pray you, Richard—"

He stopped so suddenly that she almost bumped into him. "Georgie, do go to your room. I do not want to upset you further."

She bit her lip. "Promise you will be careful?"

"Always, dearest." He kissed her forehead. "I will come to visit you later."

Richard strode down the corridor and was through the door in a flash. Georgiana waited until he was out of sight and then followed. He was angry enough to do something foolish. He also seemed to know what Mr. Wickham might want to discuss—which means they were keeping some kind of secret from her. She did not like that idea.

Georgiana emerged from the back of the house in time to see Richard advance through the garden. This part of the garden was arranged with formal, manicured beds of plants carved into interesting geometric shapes by many crisscrossing gravel paths. Mr. Wickham sat on a stone bench in front of a shallow lily pond, which was framed by small pine trees, but he was not alone. Apparently in the brief span of time since Georgiana had removed herself from his presence, Anne, an upstairs maid, had somehow wandered into his sights. Whatever Mr. Wickham whispered in her ear made Anne blush, but the stiffness in her body suggested that the attention was not welcome. *Well, at least Richard will rescue her virtue*, Georgiana thought sourly.

With a stern look, Richard sent Anne scurrying gratefully back to the house. As she brushed past, Georgiana stopped the girl with a wave. "Please send Mr. Darcy down here as quickly as possible." The maid's eyes grew wide, and she nodded before rushing to the door.

Richard said something to Mr. Wickham, but Georgiana was too far away to hear. The other man answered with an insolent shrug and a smirk. Georgiana shuddered and increased her pace. The other man did not understand how Richard's temper balanced on the edge of a knife. Indeed, the other man's irreverent attitude angered Richard, causing him to grab the front of the man's jacket.

Georgiana started to run, hoping to reach the pair before violence erupted, but it was too late. Faster than she would have thought possible, Richard punched Mr. Wickham in the jaw, causing him to fly backward and land…in the lily pond.

Chapter Ten

His body made an impressive splash, sloshing water onto the surrounding gravel. Fortunately for Mr. Wickham, the pond was very shallow, so he did not sink in very far, but his clothes were almost completely soaked. Still, she stopped to savor the astonishment on his face. *If only I could have a portrait painted of it.*

By the time she reached the edge of the pond, Mr. Wickham was flailing around in the water, succeeding at making himself wetter but not making any progress toward escaping. Georgiana could not prevent her laughter, although she concealed it behind a hand.

Finally, Mr. Wickham sat up, displaying a lily pad draped over one ear. "Damn you, Fitzwilliam!" Richard loomed over the pond's edge, practically daring the other man to emerge for another round of fisticuffs. "You are a fool if you think this changes anything. I don't fear you!"

Richard pointed with a threatening, outstretched arm. "Stay away from Georgiana!"

Mr. Wickham smirked as he removed a water plant from his sleeve. "I am afraid I cannot do that. It is my business, too, after all."

A sidelong glance confirmed that Richard was aware of her presence. He glared at Mr. Wickham. "That is enough from you!"

Georgiana was about to ask what they meant, but she was distracted by a commotion coming from the direction of the house. William strode toward them, followed by two footmen and Mr. Bennet and his wife, who was shrieking. "Why are you killing Mr. Wickham?" she demanded querulously. "He is my Lydia's beloved husband! And we require him to protect us from the French!"

Georgiana rolled her eyes and refrained from opining that Mr. Bennet could probably defend her from the French more effectively than Mr. Wickham.

A moment later, Mrs. Wickham emerged from the house, giving an anguished cry and hurrying toward the pond.

William scowled at both men. "What is going on here?"

Scrutinizing the empty garden, Mrs. Bennet threw her arms in the air. "It is the French! We are being invaded. Oh, what shall we do?"

Rogers, one of the footmen, scanned their surroundings in alarm as if expecting soldiers to jump out from behind the boxwoods at any moment.

"Mr. Bennet," William said from between clenched teeth, "perhaps now would be a good time for the sleeping draught the doctor left behind when he last examined your wife?"

"I take your point," Mr. Bennet murmured. He put an arm around his wife. "Mrs. Bennet, we are very exposed here; perhaps it is safer inside the house?"

"How true!" Mrs. Bennet pivoted and hurried back down the pathway so quickly that she practically pulled her husband behind her.

Mrs. Wickham, meanwhile, had reached the pond. "Oh, poor Wicky!" she cried as she waded into the water without any concern for her skirts. Grabbing her husband's head, she pulled it against her bosom, which was straining to escape her bodice. "Are you very hurt?" she asked breathlessly. "Is anything broken? Did you lose consciousness?"

"Only a little bruised," Mr. Wickham assured her as he stared assiduously at the view afforded by the proximity to her bodice.

William scowled at Richard. "I told you I would deal with Wickham."

"He tried to speak with Georgiana," Richard explained.

William swore loudly and switched his glare to Mr. Wickham. Striding to the edge of the pond, he leaned over and grabbed the man by his cravat, pulling him upright and out of his wife's embrace.

"What the hell are you up to?" he demanded as he shook the dripping man.

"Don't kill him! Don't strangle him!" Lydia shrieked.

Wickham smirked, although he had to be running out of air. "I believed Georgiana should be aware of the stakes as well," he rasped

"You bastard!" William cried and threw the other man to the ground at his feet. Red-faced, her brother then turned to Georgiana. "I apologize for my language." She nodded. It was hardly the most disturbing element of this tableau.

Lydia had splashed out of the pond and was prostrate by her husband's side, contributing to an ever-growing puddle of water on the lawn. "He is all wet! The poor lamb. He is sure to catch his death of cold."

William made an inarticulate growl of rage. "Rogers, Gerson," he said to the footmen through gritted teeth. "Please take Mr. Wickham inside. Ask Mrs. Reynolds to find him dry clothing and then send him back to Lambton."

Between the two of them, the footmen managed to get the sopping, stumbling mess of a man shambling toward the house. Lydia trailed disconsolately behind them, wailing as if she were the one who had been knocked into a pond.

William turned as if to follow, but Georgiana put herself in his path. "What is this all about, Brother?"

He shook his head grimly. "Nothing you need fret about."

Georgiana crossed her arms, refusing to move. "I find that difficult to believe. Mr. Wickham wished to talk with me about something. What was it?"

"I will handle it."

She shot another accusing glare at Richard. "And you know the matter as well, do you not?"

Richard looked pained. "Has it occurred to you that you might be better off if you do not know?"

She glanced from her brother to Richard and back again. "Has it occurred to you that I might imagine the problem to be worse than the reality?"

Richard and William exchanged a look. "She has a point," Richard said.

"No." William scowled.

"She is no longer a child."

William's scowl deepened. "No."

Richard folded his arms over his chest. "The matter does concern her." The two men stared at each other for what seemed like an eternity.

Finally, William gave an impatient wave. "You may tell her if you wish. And you may deal with the hysterics afterward." With that he turned and strode toward the house.

Richard frowned as he watched his cousin leave. "He is not himself. I do not know what is the matter."

Georgiana shook her head. She did not know either, but she would not allow Richard to avoid the topic at hand.

"What did Mr. Wickham threaten William with?" she demanded from Richard.

"How do you know he issued threats?"

Georgiana rolled her eyes. "I know the man. He is always after money. What did he threaten to do?"

Richard rubbed his chin, his eyes sliding away from her face. "He said…" Richard swallowed. "He claimed…" He shook his head.

"Damnation! This is hard to talk about! Pardon my language, Georgiana."

She waved the apology away. "Mr. Wickham seems to inspire it." There was silence as he struggled to articulate his thoughts. "Richard?" she prompted.

"Devil take it!" Richard heaved a big sigh. "He threatened to reveal that you had…passed the night together…that you are not…pure."

Georgiana gasped, unable to catch her breath as if she had been punched in the stomach. "That is not true!"

With two steps Richard crossed the distance between them, taking both of her forearms in his hands. "I know, dearest. He is telling tales. But someone might believe them. You *were* alone together at Ramsgate."

"Nothing happened," she said faintly, swaying a little on her feet. "Oh, merciful heavens!" Richard hastily put an arm around her shoulders and guided her to a nearby bench.

"We will not allow him to spread such lies," Richard murmured as he smoothed her hair. The gesture never failed to soothe her.

"How much has he demanded?" she asked, leaning in to Richard's touch.

"Do not worry—"

She interrupted "How much?"

He sighed. "Wickham wants your dowry."

A tear trickled down her cheek. She could usually conceal her emotions, but this news had taken her unaware. "This is all my fault. I did not see him for what he truly was…and now my dowry will be gone, and no man will marry me. And I will be a burden to William and Elizabeth!"

"Shh." The touch of his hand in her hair helped her calm down. "We shall not give him your dowry. You would never be a burden at Pemberley. And there will always be someone who will marry you, no matter your circumstances."

How could he possibly believe there is someone who will always marry me no matter what? The cynical voice in Georgiana's head laughed at the idea. *He is simply trying to reassure me; it means nothing.*

"If you do not give him my dowry, how will you stop him?" She could not prevent her voice from cracking.

"We will find a way," Richard murmured.

In other words, they have no idea, Georgiana realized.

Richard sat next to her on the bench, and she leaned toward him, resting her head on his shoulder. He continued to stroke her hair; her eyes drifted closed as she enjoyed the sensations.

The sound of a throat clearing startled her. Her head snapped up, and she found Lord Robert standing over them. They must have been so involved in their conversation that they did not hear him approach! *How do we look to him? Does it seem improper?* Richard quickly withdrew his arm from her shoulders, and Georgiana leaned away from him. The viscount nodded to them, his expression unreadable. "Miss Darcy. Colonel."

They murmured greetings back.

"I believe the men are bringing in the yule log if you care to see it." Lord Robert's eyes darted between Georgiana and Richard.

"Oh yes!" Georgiana sprang up, her eyes bright. "I always love to see the yule log." She hurried up the path, happy to have an excuse to dispel a potentially awkward situation. Of course, Richard was her cousin, so there was no impropriety in having him offer her a hug. So why did she feel they had something to hide?

***

In many houses the largest fireplace was in the front hall or the dining room, but Pemberley's happened to be in the saloon behind the marble hall. It was an enormous fireplace indeed—tall enough that one of the shorter maids could stand inside it and wide enough to fit a settee, with a chair or two at the side. This year's yule log was a magnificent specimen, a massive section of an oak tree's trunk wrapped in festive holly boughs.

By the time they had it situated in the spacious fireplace, the four farmhands were panting and wiping their brows. Elizabeth was grateful to see Mrs. Reynolds standing by with a tray of beer mugs—the men's reward for their hard labor. At least one small thing was proceeding as it should.

The farmhands laughed and joked with William and his steward, Mr. Markham, as the other guests gradually wandered into the saloon. Richard was quickly drawn into the banter when he arrived. On the other hand, Lady Catherine and Lord Robert regarded the small knot of people with disapproval. *Apparently William is too "familiar" with his tenants. Well, her approval is hardly necessary.*

When all the beer had been consumed, the farmhands tramped out. The room was still quite full—not only of family and guests, but many of the servants had also joined them to observe the lighting of the yule log. *How lovely*, Elizabeth thought. *Christmas is an occasion when the distinctions of rank do not need to be so rigidly preserved.*

Lady Catherine shot William a meaningful look and tilted her head toward the door, suggesting that the servants should depart. The master of Pemberley regarded his aunt quizzically as if he did not comprehend her meaning. Elizabeth choked back a laugh.

Before his aunt could importune him any further, William's attention was drawn by Mrs. Reynolds, who had produced the piece of charcoal left over from the previous year's yule log. *Trust her to ensure the tradition is observed!* William lit the charcoal with all due ceremony and then used it to ignite the enormous log in the fireplace. As the log blazed into a healthy fire, many of the observers clapped with delight. The log was expected to burn until Twelfth Night. A scullery maid would rest at the hearth and, in exchange for a handsome bonus, ensure the fire did not die out during the night.

The staff lingered to talk after the ceremony was complete, and William seemed in no rush to hurry them out of the room. Clearly this was part of the ritual as well. Finally, they all drifted away, and only family and friends remained, clustered around the fireplace. "Now that is what I call a good blaze!" Richard declared.

"Indeed," Elizabeth's father said. "We have no fireplace at Longbourn large enough for a true yule log. This is quite a treat."

"When I am in residence at Rosings Park," Lady Catherine exclaimed, "we have yule logs in *two* fireplaces."

Elizabeth happened to notice Georgiana, who rolled her eyes dramatically. At least she was not allowing Lady Catherine's sourness to ruin her Christmas spirit.

Edging a little closer to the fireplace, Elizabeth basked in the heat it created. As her skin absorbed the warmth, it eased the knot of tension in her stomach. It was as if the yule log had magical soothing properties. She was unaware of William's presence beside her until an arm encircled her shoulders—and she took advantage of the opportunity to lean against his reassuring, solid weight. The fire created an ever-changing pattern of light and shadow that was quite mesmerizing. William pulled her closer to his side. "Happy Christmas, my love."

Perhaps everything would be all right. At least in this moment they could enjoy the Christmas warmth together. "Happy Christmas, darling," she replied.

Georgiana clapped her hands. "We should play a game before dinner!"

"Oh yes!" Lydia squealed. "A game would be most fun!"

"A game?" Lady Catherine's tone could not have been more disdainful if Georgiana had announced a desire to eat insects. "Games are for children and the lower classes." Noticing her sister-in-law's downcast eyes, Elizabeth wondered if she should intercede.

William cleared his throat loudly. "At Pemberley we always play games on Christmas Eve. What would you like, Georgie?"

His sister lifted her head and gave him a grin. "How about blind man's buff?"

Lady Catherine opened her mouth to object, but William did not give her an opportunity. "That would be delightful," he said hastily, gesturing to his cousin and the other young men. "Let us reposition the furniture to create room. Nobody wants bruised shins as a souvenir of their visit to Pemberley. Mrs. Reynolds, do you have something that could be used as a blindfold?"

It was only a matter of minutes until they had rearranged tables and settees to create a clear space in the center of the room. Lady Catherine and Elizabeth's parents remained seated, but everyone else was taking part.

William held up the blindfold. "Who shall be our first player?"

Lydia leapt forward eagerly, but Mrs. Bennet called out, "It must be someone unmarried! My mother always said that the first player at blind man's buff would catch his or her true love."

Elizabeth rolled her eyes at the repetition of this silly superstition. "Mama—"

"Very well," William said. "Georgiana shall be the first player."

His sister's face lost all color as she regarded him. *What was he thinking? Georgiana had two suitors among the players.* Her mother's pronouncement might be a silly superstition, but it had raised the stakes for a simple game.

"Very well." Georgiana's voice was strangled. She marched over to her brother as if to the gallows. Looking a bit chagrined, William tied the blindfold around her eyes, turned her around three times, and then backed away.

Georgiana groped around in space, trying to find the others while they shouted and laughed, giving her voices to follow. However, it was immediately apparent that while William, Lydia, and Elizabeth were doing their best not to be caught, the same could not be said for Mr. Worthy and the viscount. They glared daggers at each other as they made feeble attempts to evade Georgiana's reach, but neither ventured very far from her vicinity. Apparently neither man was averse to being characterized as Georgiana's true love. *Oh, for Heaven's sake!*

Richard's behavior was the most interesting of all, however. He was less obvious about his maneuvering than the other two men, yet somehow he was constantly the closest to Georgiana. His never-ending stream of encouraging remarks also helped her to discern his location. He was playing an entirely different game from the others.

The end, when it came, was swift. Lord Robert had put himself in Georgiana's path rather obviously, retreating only incrementally. Nevertheless, Mr. Worthy's foot somehow ended up behind the viscount's, causing Lord Robert to sprawl backward onto the carpet. Since the man's demise was silent, Georgiana continued on her path, running the risk of stumbling over the viscount's legs and doing herself injury. At the last moment, Richard interposed himself, allowing his cousin to run right into his chest.

"Oomph!" Georgiana exclaimed. "Who is this?" She ran her hands over the sleeves of his coat and then pulled off her blindfold. "Richard!"

Why did this prompt such a furious blush? Elizabeth wondered.

"I will always come to your rescue, Cuz." Richard gave her a quick kiss on the cheek. They locked eyes for just a second, but it was long enough. Elizabeth's epiphany struck quickly. *Oh. I see.*

"Well, that is no good!" Elizabeth's mother cried from the other side of the room. "He is her cousin, not her true love!"

Richard instantly released Georgiana's arm as if she had burned him and backed away. Elizabeth shushed Mrs. Bennet. "He saved her from tripping," she observed. "Even though it cost him the game."

Georgiana's eyes were still fixed on her cousin. "Quite the noble sacrifice," she said faintly. She took two steps toward him and handed him the blindfold. "Well, now it is your turn Richard. Can you be faster than I?"

***

Richard captured Darcy, and then Darcy caught Elizabeth—who ensnared Lydia rather handily. At that point, the entire party was obligated to quit the game and dress for dinner. But it was agreed—by all but Aunt Catherine—that the amusement had been excessively diverting.

Richard changed his clothes with alacrity and soon found himself in the drawing room adjoining Pemberley's formal dining room. Staring out the window, Georgiana was the only other occupant. And there was a kissing bough over the doorway. The sight of the two together in an otherwise empty room caused his insides to agitate as if he were about to ride into battle.

It was the perfect opportunity to learn more about her sentiments, but she had already been accosted—twice—under kissing boughs. Richard did not want to be added to the list of unwelcome advances.

On the other hand, after his conversation with Darcy, Richard had pondered whether something between him and Georgiana was indeed possible. By this point he understood his own sentiments quite well, but how would he ever ascertain hers?

Did she prefer the viscount? Had that been a flash of disappointment on her face when she realized that she had caught him rather than Lord Robert? Was he asking too much to hope she might ever view him as more than a friend?

Well, there was one way to find out, although Richard's hands shook and his stomach seemed to be attempting to leave his body. *I faced Napoleon's troops. I can face this.* He positioned himself under the kissing bough and plucked one of the mistletoe berries. "Look what I have." He held his palm flat so she could glimpse the berry.

Georgiana's gaze darted from his face to the berry and back again. "I think I am owed a kiss." He mustered what he hoped was his most charming smile. How would she react?

Georgiana blinked several times and then walked slowly toward him, her eyes never wavering from his. When only a foot separated them, she stretched out her hand, and he dropped the berry into it.

Richard's gaze slipped from her eyes to her mouth. Those luxuriant pink lips, so full and soft. What would such a kiss feel like? His hands twitched with the need to pull her closer, but he dared not scare her away. He must await her move.

Following her gaze, he found it fixed on his mouth. Surely that was a hopeful sign? "Richard..." she breathed, her voice caressing the syllables of his name. But would she tell him to go to hell?

She leaned forward. Her breath brushed his cheek…

The room's stillness was punctured by the sound of approaching voices. "Mama, do not tell me what to do! I am a grown woman!" Mrs. Wickham's peevish tones echoed wildly from the marble hall.

Damnation! If they had only been two minutes later…

Georgiana's mouth darted to the side of his face for a quick peck on his cheek. "Happy Christmas, Richard," she murmured.

"Happy Christmas," he returned as the Bennets trooped into the drawing room. He scrutinized Georgiana's face, but it was shuttered off, revealing none of her feelings.

He had learned nothing.

Chapter Eleven

Darcy regretted losing the opportunity to spend Christmas alone with his wife, but he was forced to admit that there was something cheery about a tableful of guests. The candles created a soft glow, gleaming off the china and silver. Boughs of evergreens and holly adorned the walls, and mistletoe hung over the doors. The fat Christmas candle sat squarely in the middle of the table. According to tradition, it must burn from now until Christmas night, or the family would have bad luck. Darcy did not believe in the superstition, but the candle's golden light brought back fond memories of celebrating Christmas as a child.

Since Pemberley would be hosting others for dinner on Christmas Day, the family was having their Christmas feast that night. Cook had outdone herself with venison and turkey as well as potatoes, beans, and apples. For the sweets course, they would have plum pudding and march pane. Such a festive atmosphere would not exist without guests to feed and entertain.

"I do not hold with having a Christmas candle," Aunt Catherine announced. "It is a papist tradition, you know."

Of course, guests can be valued too highly.

Elizabeth frowned. "I do not believe so."

The older woman nodded sagely. "I learned it from—"

"If it is papist tradition, it might be French!" Mrs. Bennet exclaimed, apparently oblivious to having interrupted a peer of the realm. She waved her handkerchief about. "Do you think French candles are quite safe?"

Darcy attempted his most soothing voice. "I assure you, madam, this candle was made in England." His mother-in-law continued to view the item dubiously as if it might explode at any moment. Darcy was not amused.

"Wicky would love this," Lydia pouted. "I do not see why he must remain at that dismal inn all alone."

Darcy's patience with the Wickhams had been exhausted. "You may join him there," he told Lydia.

She slumped back into her chair without any sign she had heard him. "It is so unfair." Then her eyes widened, and she sat up. "La! More venison!" Leaning across the table, she served herself meat from a platter on the other side.

Darcy noticed the impending disaster a second before it happened but could not prevent it. Lydia's eager arm brushed the Christmas candle, knocking it completely out of its holder and onto the tablecloth.

And that was how Lydia set Pemberley on fire for a second time.

**

William looked quite weary, sitting before the fire in his study with a glass of port in one hand and a book in the other. Although he had changed out of his soot-stained clothing, a smudge of black still graced the hand that held the port. Rather than reading, however, he stared at the flames in the fireplace. Elizabeth wondered if he was recalling the blaze that had destroyed Pemberley's dining table. Unlike the fire in Lydia's bedchamber, the one in the dining room had taken some time to extinguish.

The tablecloth had caught the flame like a torch, and part of the table itself had been burned. In the process of extinguishing the blaze, William, Richard, and the staff had broken several pieces of crystal and china. Needless to say, Cook's lovely dinner had been ruined.

Lydia did not even have the grace to apologize. Giggling occasionally, she had merely observed as others handled a potentially deadly situation. William had shown admirable restraint in not banishing Lydia from Pemberley on the spot.

Embarrassment had prevented Elizabeth from discussing her family with William, but she now knew it was unavoidable. Taking a deep breath, she drew close to the fireplace and sank into the chair next to William's. He gave her a wan smile and took a sip from his glass.

"How are you?" she asked.

He dropped the book into his lap and ran his free hand through his hair. "Weary. Despite having taken a bath, I still smell like smoke. I may require another bath before retiring for the night."

"My mother always says surprises are good at Christmas time." Elizabeth gave him a mischievous grin. Perhaps they could laugh about their mishaps.

William frowned. "Hmm…many more of those kinds of surprises might kill me."

Elizabeth's smile slid away. She swallowed, clenching her hands tightly in her lap. "I…I wish to apologize."

"For what?" One of William's eyebrows quirked upward.

"My family. They imposed on your hospitality, and now they are the source of endless trouble."

William's brow furrowed. "It is *our* hospitality since it is *our* home. And they are causing *you* at least as much trouble as they cause me."

She knew this was true—in theory. "But I am still sorry for all the inconveniences."

"I do not hold you responsible." His voice was gentle.

It should have been a relief to hear those words, but she could not help believing she had brought this trouble and mortification into his life. Her family had embarrassed William myriad times in the presence of his cousin and aunt—not to mention a peer of the realm. *How could he forgive me for that? Can I forgive myself?*

Acknowledging that her relatives were beyond Elizabeth's control would not prevent him from regretting that he had ever married her. Such regret was her greatest fear. Recently, he had grown so taciturn and ill-tempered. What else could be the cause?

She finally ventured to glance at his face, but it was carefully blank, granting no reassurance. As a yawn overtook her, she stood. "Will you come to bed?" Perhaps they could come to a kind of understanding in each other's arms. She craved the comfort and security of his body enveloping hers.

The flames of the fire seemed to mesmerize him. "Not now. I need additional time before retiring. But you should sleep. I will be along in a little while."

Elizabeth nodded and stood. She fled the room as silently as she could as if her footfalls were the source of William's disquiet.

She had failed.

William had claimed to accept her apology, but obviously he had not.

What will I do now?

Chapter Twelve

Christmas Day was quite a bit colder than Christmas Eve. The Darcy family and their guests attended morning services at Kympton church and returned home for a light luncheon. As was the tradition, Darcy had invited tenants and other locals to Pemberley for an afternoon of food and merriment for the entire neighborhood. It was an opportunity for the Darcy family to set aside class boundaries and forge bonds with their neighbors over their shared joy about the holiday.

Georgiana loved the tradition, although Lady Catherine had sniffed disapprovingly about the unwashed peasantry haunting the halls of Pemberley and issued dire warnings about locking up the silver. William had dismissed her concerns by observing that many of the poorer families in the neighborhood relied upon the Darcy family's tradition for their Christmas cheer. Without a visit to Pemberley, they would not have a happy Christmas. Sniffing again, Lady Catherine had declared she would not attend the event; William had admirably refrained from observing that no one would miss her.

Elizabeth and Georgiana had supervised the preparations. The ballroom was bedecked with evergreens and holly and twinkling candles. A few of the locals would be playing instruments, and some dancing was to be expected. Inevitably groups of wassailers would also form, traveling throughout the crowds and singing.

Georgiana mentally reviewed all of the preparations. Did they have enough of the small toys for all of the children who might visit? Were there sufficient apples to bob for apples? Would they need more turkey? She was pleased and relieved to share the responsibilities for the open house with Elizabeth. They had planned and prepared together, but—being more sociably inclined—Elizabeth would act as hostess during the event itself.

The ballroom boasted tables laden with turkey, goose, beans, potatoes, and various kinds of breads as well as punch bowl full of wassail and plum pudding for dessert. To the delight of the children, a small table was even devoted to gingerbread. Preparations occupied the staff for several days before Christmas, although it put everyone in a cheerful mood.

It was the lull before the storm. Georgiana had sought refuge in the library before the guests descended upon Pemberley. Richard had already been ensconced in a chair, reading a historical tome, and

Georgiana had joined him in companionable silence as she settled down with a volume of poetry.

In the quiet, the rattle of an opening door startled her. Lord Robert walked in. "There you are, Miss Darcy! Nobody seems knowledgeable about your whereabouts." He spared Richard an irritated glance as if her cousin had somehow been concealing her.

Georgiana closed her book. "How may I be of service, Lord Robert?"

His smile lit his entire face, reminding her that he was a most handsome man. "You had promised me a tour of the formal gardens if the weather was nice."

Well, now was as good a time as any. "I suppose there is time before the guests arrive." Georgiana stood, brushing the wrinkles from her dress. She could grab her shawl from a nearby table.

Richard stood as well, a strange, unreadable expression on his face. "Today *would* be a beautiful day to view the gardens," he said, glancing through the library's French doors at the sculpted shrubbery beyond.

Georgiana had a brief, panicked vision of awkwardly touring the gardens with both men. Why did they always seem at odds? They had never uttered an uncivil word to each other in her hearing, yet an undercurrent of animosity suffused their interactions.

Lord Robert was frowning at something. Following his gaze, Georgiana saw her pistol and practice target on a table where she had hastily disposed of them when she entered the house yesterday.

"Practicing with your pistol, Colonel?" the viscount drawled to Richard. "It is not good form to leave weapons lying about when there are ladies present."

Richard stiffened but merely nodded. "Yes, very careless of me."

He was dissembling for her sake, and Georgiana would not allow it. She could easily recall Aunt Catherine's voice admonishing her about ladylike behavior, but she ignored it. "Actually, my lord, the pistol is mine. I was doing some target practice yesterday."

The expression the viscount turned on her could only be described as stupefied. "I heard that you shoot pistols. But why do target practice?"

She shrugged. "Amusement, just as with many gentlemen."

"B-but surely you do not hunt," he spluttered.

"No. I do not care for it."

"But she can decimate any clay targets you toss in the air," Richard chimed in.

Lord Robert's face demonstrated that he did not believe Richard. His gaze lowered to the paper target she had used the day before. "Quite a commendable effort, Miss Darcy."

Georgiana gritted her teeth. He was humoring her; some of the bullets had not been dead center. "It is not so bad for my left hand, but I have had better days."

Lord Robert's eyes grew large. "You shot that with your left hand?"

She shrugged. "The target was not so far. It would hardly have been a challenge with my right."

Richard managed not to laugh, but his eyes were dancing. Clearly he enjoyed the lord's discomfiture. "It is a shame Georgie is a woman," he said. "With her skills at riding and shooting, she would have made an excellent soldier."

Georgiana shuddered. "I am just as happy to skip the marching and fighting, thank you."

Lord Robert regarded her with a slightly glazed expression—as if his image of her was reshaping itself before her eyes. She experienced another pang of self-doubt and regret. No. She straightened her spine. *This is who I am.* "Are you ready for your tour?" she asked the viscount.

He shook off his reverie. "Certainly."

Richard gave a quick bow. "I will leave you to it. I have some correspondence which requires attention."

Georgiana had a momentary impulse to beg him to stay, although she could not for the life of her say why. Certainly she was capable of giving a tour of the gardens without his help. Nevertheless, she felt hollow and empty when the door closed behind him.

"Where shall we go first?" Lord Robert asked, offering her his arm and opening one of the French doors.

Georgiana pointed. "Perhaps the trellises on the south side of the garden. There are no blooms, but the vines are magnificent..."

***

Richard forced his feet to plod along the hallway's parquet floor— and tried to stifle the mental voice screaming that he should retrace his steps and stand between Georgiana and the too-wealthy, too-attractive lord. Instead he ground his teeth and quickened his pace. The further he was from them, the further from temptation.

This is better for Georgiana. Lord Robert is the kind of man she deserves. They will get to know each other as they tour the garden. If in a month or so, he asks her to marry him, she will be spared the trouble of a season—as well as the indignities of Wickham's accusations. *That would be a good thing,* he reminded himself sternly. *Georgiana's happiness is paramount, not my futile, moonstruck fantasies.*

He could not help recalling the ghostly sensation of her breath on his cheek when he thought they might kiss under the mistletoe. *In all likelihood she was simply humoring me and never had any other idea than a quick peck on the cheek.*

This silent monologue continued as he climbed the stairs and entered his bedchamber. But once he had flung himself on his bed, heedless of his clothing, a terrible thought struck him. Georgiana and the viscount were alone, outside, unchaperoned. Richard believed the man to be honorable, someone who would not take advantage of the situation. *But what if Lord Robert took the occasion of their solo stroll to make her an offer?*

Good Lord, no! I must stop him. Richard jumped to his feet and strode toward the door, but his hand froze on the doorknob. *I want Georgie to be happy. This is best for her.* She will marry a fine, upstanding nobleman—and would never know that Richard had had more than cousinly feelings for her.

It took a great effort of will to release the doorknob, but he forced his fingers apart. Then he backed away from the door, each step like wading through neck-deep water. *This is best for Georgie,* he reminded himself again and again. *Damnation!* He plunged fingers into his hair, tugging at the roots as if the slight pain would help him focus. *When did I grow so blasted indecisive? I am a soldier; I should know what I want.* However, this realization did nothing to bring clarity.

He sat at the desk, resolved to concentrate on his correspondence; however, only two minutes' time was required to demonstrate the futility of that endeavor. He needed a different distraction. Perhaps a bracing ride. Or a game of billiards. He flung the door open and marched toward the stairs.

William stood at the top step, staring into space. To state the obvious, this was not his cousin's usual state of mind. "Is there a problem?" Richard asked.

William's hair was an unruly mess, and his eyes were shadowed as he turned toward Richard. "No. Well, yes. Have you seen Lord Robert?"

"I just left him with Georgiana. He asked for a tour of the garden."

"He did?" William's eyebrows shot up. "Did he seem...agitated at all?"

"Not particularly. Why?"

William's lips twisted in disgust. "I just learned from Giles that yesterday Wickham talked with him. The footmen left Wickham in a bedroom to change into some dry clothing. When they returned, Wickham was in earnest conversation with the viscount. Perhaps Wickham wishes to demonstrate how harmful gossip could be if I do not accede to his blackmail."

Richard's mouth dropped open. "He would not dare—"

William snorted. "This is Wickham. Of course he would. He would like nothing better than to ruin Georgiana's hopes of marriage by spreading rumors of her 'scandalous past.'"

"Damn the man!" Richard slammed a fist down on the banister. "I would dearly love to thrash him."

"He has been banished from Pemberley, but it occurred to me that he might try to slip in with the townspeople from Lambton." William gave him a small wave. "I do not condone thrashing, but you have my permission to evict him from the premises." Richard nodded.

William's gaze traveled down the stairs. "Should I go out to the garden?"

Richard frowned. "Why?" Did he not wish Lord Robert to propose?

"The viscount might mention Wickham's accusations to Georgiana."

Richard could easily picture the anguished expression on her exquisite face. "Would he do such a thing?"

William frowned. "I do not know the man well enough to say." They exchanged a troubled glance, a silent message passing between them. Then, as one, they raced down the stairs, strode through the marble hall, and hurried along the corridor to the back door. However, Richard stopped William before he opened the door. "Perhaps it is best if I talk with Lord Robert. Alone. She is your sister, and you are very close to the situation. I certainly know enough of the particulars to refute any accusations."

William glowered, but his cousin continued to block the master of Pemberley from the door. Finally, William's shoulders slumped. "Very well. I suppose we do not want to descend on the man like a pack of hunting dogs. I will be in my study if he should wish to speak with me."

The words sent a shudder through Richard. Of course, there were many reasons Lord Robert might wish for a private word with William but one in particular that concerned Richard. No. "Concerned" was too weak a word. "Terrified" was more accurate.

William turned back toward the marble hall and was soon gone from sight. Richard stared at the back door, envisioning how he would explain Wickham's lies to Lord Robert. Still, a part of him wanted to reject this plan. Richard did not want to smooth the path for the nobleman. In fact, he wanted the nobleman to drown in the lily pond.

If Lord Robert understood how Wickham's accusations sprang from his animosity, he might dismiss them—and then propose to Georgiana. Richard would vastly prefer that the viscount propose to some other lady far away from Derbyshire. No. He squared his shoulders. He could never allow anyone to believe untrue things about Georgie; he cared too much.

Richard gave the inoffensive wooden door before him the evil eye as if it were responsible for his dilemma. He just wanted what was best for Georgie, but what was that? Well, there was only one way he could find out. Richard took a deep breath.

Just as he reached for the knob, the door opened, and Georgiana slipped through.

Chapter Thirteen

The entire time Georgiana was telling Lord Robert about boxwoods and pointing out laurels she suspected his mind was elsewhere. His eyes went where she pointed, and he made appreciative noises, but he did not appear to be fully engaged in the activity. Finally, they returned once more to the lily pond. Georgiana seated herself on the bench, shrugging her shawl more tightly around her shoulders. It was warm for December, but the air still had a bite in it. Lord Robert placed himself beside her.

"I am pleased we have a moment of privacy." His face was very solemn.

Oh. She had a suspicion what was next. Georgiana's heart started pounding with dread. Hmm…perhaps that sensation of dread indicated something about how she should respond to his words.

He took one of her gloved hands in his. "I wished to tell you how I have come to admire you over these past few days and…" His tongue moistened dry lips. "…to beg you to be my wife." Lord Robert's smile was a placid expression. Should he not be more excited about the prospect of marriage to her?

"Um." How should she respond?

"You are a very lovely young lady," he continued, although his eyes did not meet hers. They seemed fixed on a distant point past her right shoulder. "And I am certain you will make a wonderful wife and mother once you settle down."

Georgiana blinked, the sensation of dread suddenly becoming much more acute. "Settle down?"

He gave her a gentle smile. "Well…we do have our differences."

She knitted her brow. "I do not have the pleasure of understanding you."

"You…er, ride horses like a man and shoot pistols like a man." His tone suggested the answer was obvious.

"So you are saying we are too much *alike*."

"No! Er…yes…I suppose." He scowled. "But certainly you do not intend to pursue these sorts of *activities*"—his lip curled as if the word was blasphemy—"once you are married."

Something constricted in Georgiana's chest. Give them up? No more target practice? Riding sidesaddle for the rest of her life? Would *any* potential husband expect that from her? A cold sweat broke out on the back of her neck. Was this was the best offer that she could hope for?

She itched to reject this offer; surely remaining a spinster would be preferable to such a union. But there was the matter of Mr. Wickham and the threat to her dowry. If she accepted Lord Robert and married him immediately, surely it would be too soon for the scoundrel to enact his plan. She and her dowry would be safe from him.

But at what price?

A man who loves you would not seek to make you change. Elizabeth's words resonated in her mind. Aside from her beloved brother, there was only one man who accepted her as she was. And she loved him for it.

The truth washed over her like a bucket of cold water. *Oh! I am* in love *with him.* Her eyes opened to the sight of Lord Robert's patient, hopeful face. *What an inconvenient time for* that *revelation.*

She swallowed. *How awkward.* But there was no point in prolonging the discussion. No matter the consequences for her dowry, she could not accept a proposal from one man while pining for another. "Lord Robert, I am honored by your offer, but I am afraid I must decline."

He gaped. Had he been so certain of his acceptance? "But you cannot be assured that you will receive another offer from a man who will tolerate your eccentricities."

He called that tolerance? Her anxiety mutated into anger. "Then I will be an old maid," she told him through clenched teeth. "Quite happily."

"Surely any union between us would be a happy one!" he pleaded, grasping her hand. "We are compatible in so many ways."

She pulled her hand away and moved discreetly down the bench. "I do not perceive us to be compatible in the most important ways."

The viscount's face fell, and his shoulders lowered fractionally. "I have made you angry. That was not my intention, and I apologize." He would not meet her eyes. "Perhaps it would be best if I return to the house now."

Georgiana nodded. "I thank you for the honor of your address and hope we can continue to be friends."

He nodded stiffly and then stood, observing the house for a moment before glancing down at her. "I had a rather odd conversation with Mr. Wickham yesterday." His voice was now rather conversational.

"Oh?" Georgiana stiffened. *What lies had that scoundrel told?*

"He spun a quite unbelievable, outrageous story about you." The lord's eyes narrowed, and his lips twisted.

"He did?" Georgiana widened her eyes as if she could not imagine what Mr. Wickham would say.

"Yes, quite disgusting. As if you would ever carry on with a man like that." The lord brushed a speck of dust from his coat. "But you should tell your brother about Mr. Wickham. Something must be done to check his callous disregard for the truth."

"Of course," Georgiana said faintly.

"I bid you good day." Lord Robert gave her a brief bow and was gone.

Georgiana rose slowly from the bench and wandered toward the house, her mind full of Lord Robert's words. *I have done the right thing*, she reassured herself. He had pretended to tolerate her "odd habits," when in truth he wanted her to quit them.

But what if no other man would suffer it? There was one man who *would* gladly bear such eccentricities. Did he have interest in anything more than friendship?

Georgiana was still lost in her reverie when she reached the back door to Pemberley. She opened it hastily, nearly knocking over Richard. Startled, she stepped backward and nearly tripped. "I beg your pardon!"

He recoiled at the same moment. "So sorry, Georgie!"

Georgiana closed the door behind her. The hallway was utterly silent as they stared at each other, apparently mutually at a loss for words. It was so odd; ordinarily there was never silence between them. Georgiana could not meet Richard's eyes, and he appeared fascinated by the wall. Finally, he cleared his throat. "Um, where did Lord Robert go?"

Georgiana shrugged. "I do not know."

This drew a startled frown. "Did he…is he speaking with William?"

"I suppose he might be."

Richard's face paled, and he leaned against the wall. Georgiana took a step forward. *Was he ill?*

"Surely he does not intend to marry you without William's permission!" he exclaimed.

"Marry me?" Georgiana's voice squeaked in surprise. "We are not engaged!" How had he guessed the viscount might propose? Surely Lord Robert did not tell him.

"Oh." There was an odd expression on Richard's face. Abruptly he leaned over, his hands resting on his knees and his breath emerging in gasps as if he were recovering from a long race.

Alarm raced down Georgiana's spine. "Are you quite all right?"

Finally, her cousin straightened, a fierce light shining in his eyes. "He *should* want to marry you. You are worth ten Lord Roberts!"

Georgiana blinked. These mercurial mood swings were difficult to follow. What was troubling him? "He did propose, but I declined," she said.

"But he is very eligible and from a good family. It would be a good match."

Georgiana said the first thing that came into her head. "Do you *want* me to marry him?"

"Yes! No!" Richard buried his face in his hands. "Just shoot me now," he moaned.

"Why would I do that?" Georgiana asked. "It would hardly be sporting."

Richard's shoulders shook with silent laughter. When his hands dropped away, he was still chuckling. She waited patiently until he sobered. "Why did you refuse him?" he asked finally.

She shrugged. "He assumed I would renounce shooting and riding astride. It was an easy decision."

Richard's head thumped back against the wall. "Thank you, Lord."

What? "Richard, you are behaving very strangely. Is something wrong?"

His grin was like the sun emerging from behind a cloud. "No. Absolutely nothing is wrong. Everything is right. Absolutely, completely right!"

Now Georgiana was more confused than ever.

Richard glanced up and down the hallway, scrutinizing its nondescript walls. "Not here..." he muttered under his breath. "Let us go outside."

Georgiana was enjoying being warm for the first time in an hour, but it seemed so important to Richard that she nodded her agreement. Taking her hand in his, he gently pulled her through the doorway and into the garden.

Gravel crunched under their feet as he led her back to the bench near the pond. He helped her sit and then placed himself next to her.

However, he seemed a bit reluctant to speak. After a minute, Georgiana prompted, "Richard?"

He swallowed. "It would be easier to ride into battle," he murmured.

Anxiety prickled at the back of her neck. "Is what you have to say so awful then?"

He exhaled a laugh. "No. Not at all. I do not think..." His eyes were fixed on his hand where it clasped hers. "Dearest, I...realized something today...when I thought Lord Robert might propose to you." Georgiana noticed a tremor in her fingers. *Are my hands trembling or are his?*

His eyes rose to meet hers. "I cannot—" He hesitated for a moment and then started again. "I do not wish you to marry someone else."

She frowned. What on earth did he mean by that? She had to marry someone. Or did he believe she should be a spinster? Or was it possible...? Did she dare to hope that he might experience some fraction of the sentiments she was only now recognizing?

"I want— I have fallen—" He shook his head as if disgusted with himself and started again. "I wish I could speak with more eloquence." His eyes held hers; she could not have looked away if her life depended on it. "But the plain truth is that I am in love with you. And I would have you be my wife if you would take me. But if you say no, we will never speak of it again."

Georgiana's mouth dropped open; a small voice at the back of her mind imagined Mrs. Annesley chastising her about it. "Y-you l-love me?" she repeated. He nodded earnestly with lips set in a straight, anxious line.

"But if you do not return the feelings..." He squeezed her hand quite hard. "...I understand. I do not want this to affect our friendship."

It was wonderful in a way that Georgiana had not known anything could possibly be wonderful. As if someone had ferreted out the most secret, unspoken desire of her heart and presented it to her on a silver platter. A daydream made into reality.

She had only just realized how deeply her feelings for Richard ran. The thought that he returned even a small measure of those feelings—let alone want her as his wife—was overwhelming, like being engulfed by a wave on the beach. The announcement was so unanticipated, so sudden that a hundred different unexpressed thoughts and unasked questions all clogged her throat, making it impossible to say anything at all.

When she did not respond immediately, the animation left Richard's face. "I will speak of it no more." He tried to withdraw his hand from her grasp, but she clenched her fingers more tightly.

She opened her mouth, but only a strangled gurgle emerged. *If only I could manage to say something!*

But the words simply were not available. *If I cannot tell him, I will show him.* Georgiana leaned forward, inclined her head, and kissed Richard on the lips. It was a short kiss but sweet and gentle and full of promise, provoking a full-body shiver that had nothing to do with the cold. When she pulled back, Richard could not have looked more surprised if she had run him through with a sword.

"Is that a—" His voice faltered, and he coughed before he spoke again. "Is that a yes?"

She smiled. "Yes."

The joy on Richard's face shone so brightly it could have lit a room. Richard initiated the next kiss, a far longer and more passionate affair. His mouth caressed hers, demanding attention, insisting that she return his affections. She acquiesced joyfully. And when his tongue pushed into her mouth…she had not known that was part of kissing, but, oh, it was wonderful! The sensation of being so close, so in tune, in perfect harmony with another person—that was what had been absent in her previous kissing experiences. Richard played her mouth like a virtuoso; Mr. Wickham might as well have been a choir boy.

His hand buried itself in her hair, dislodging pins to allow silken tresses to fall about her shoulders. Her arm snaked around his waist, and still she was too far from him. She pressed her body against his, pushing her lips into his, and it was not close enough. It was as if her entire being wanted to merge with his, body and soul. *Oh,* she realized. *That is what will happen on the wedding night.* Suddenly she anticipated that event with excitement rather than dread.

Why did we waste time talking when we could have been doing this?

Finally, Richard broke it off, although his hand remained buried in her hair. They were both breathing unevenly, and Richard's face was quite red. "I had not expected…that," he murmured.

"Kissing is not always so?" Her kissing experience was very limited after all.

Richard snorted. "No." He skimmed a free hand up her arm, and she shuddered in delight. "You set me on fire."

He meant it as a compliment, yet it hardly sounded like the kind of thing a proper lady would do. Georgiana could not imagine Mrs. Annesley setting anyone on fire.

Richard's finger was under her chin, tilting her face upward, and she suddenly understood what he meant. She glowed with an inner warmth that the surrounding cold could not diminish. "Georgie, it is a good thing. Kissing you was…wonderful. Far superior to anything I had ever dreamed of. And believe me, I dreamed of it frequently."

"You did?" she asked. *Perhaps "ladylike" is not the most important quality for a kiss.*

He angled his head to meet her eyes. "However, you…I…it is important that *you* want this. I do not want you to accept me out of a sense of obligation or because you want to escape a London season or—"

She smiled. At least she knew how to respond to this. "Perhaps I shall accept you because I also have been secretly dreaming about it for the last year?" She gave him a cheeky grin.

His eyes widened. "Truly?"

She nodded. "But I did not dare hope. Oh, Richard, you have made me so happy!" She flung her arms around his waist, allowing her body to speak her elation.

He clasped her tightly against him and murmured endearments into her ear. Finally, he pulled away. "Dearest, you have made me the happiest man in England, but we are still within view of the house. Someone gazing out of a window might see something untoward…before I have a chance to talk with William and make it official."

Georgiana sighed. He was right. They should go into the house and do their duties, tell William, then the rest of the party, and receive congratulations. However, at the moment that prospect was unappealing. Right now their love and their betrothal were just for them—a private joy.

"Of course, they will all be occupied with the visitors…" She observed.

Richard barked a laugh. "I had almost forgotten it is Christmas!"

She gave him a shy smile. "When I was a child, you and William and Papa would give me presents for Christmas." Richard nodded at the memory. "I missed that tradition when I grew up—receiving Christmas presents." Her grin turned mischievous. "I am so pleased you decided to revive the tradition."

Richard looked perplexed for a moment, but then understanding dawned. He gave the back of her hand a teasing kiss. "Nay. *You* have given *me* the best present of all."

She collected the wayward hairpins and rearranged her coiffure while gazing longingly at the natural gardens past the lily pond. There they could disappear into the trees—to walk and talk and perhaps kiss... But she turned resolutely toward the house. "I suppose we should make an appearance at the festivities."

"Do you think our absence will be marked?" Richard asked. "There are so many guests."

"Well, everyone will be rather busy...and I have completed my duties," Georgiana said, glancing again at the wild garden. "Perhaps we might go for a walk? There are plenty of lovely spots which are *not* within view of the house."

His eyebrows rose. "Are there?" He stood and then tugged her into a standing position. "Perhaps we should visit them."

Chapter Fourteen

Darcy sank gratefully into a chair before the fireplace and took a sip of brandy. This moment in the study was the most relaxed Richard had seen his cousin all day. "Were the Christmas festivities well attended?" he asked.

Darcy's eyebrows rose. "You were not there?"

Richard shifted in his chair. "I had intended to be, but I was admiring the gardens and time got away from me." This was not a wholly inaccurate statement.

Darcy frowned but did not comment on Richard's uncharacteristic passion for gardens in December. "I think we had the most visitors of any year," Darcy mused. "Many were eager to meet the new Mrs. Darcy." He smiled fondly. "And she was more than equal to the task. The wassailers sang all of my favorite Christmas songs, 'Deck the Halls,' 'While Shepherds Watched Their Flocks by Night,' and 'Here We Come a-Wassailing,' naturally." He took a sip. "I suspect a spy might have informed them of my preferences."

Richard chuckled. "Was the food as good as always?" he asked.

"Delicious! Very little of it remains. The gingerbread was particularly popular with the children."

"And they did not rob you blind?" Richard asked with a grin.

Darcy laughed. "This has been the tradition for three and twenty years. We have never had a problem with theft or rowdiness. Everyone was on his or her best behavior, except for Aunt Catherine; she joined us briefly and sneered at everyone." Darcy took a sip. "Oh, and Mrs. Bennet was certain that French spies would use the event to sneak into Pemberley. No doubt she is waiting for them to attack her in her bed even now."

Richard laughed and shook his head. "I do not know how her husband copes with her."

"Neither do I." Darcy stared at the fire. "But all in all, the 'rabble' behaved better than our official guests. None of them set fire to Pemberley even once."

"I will be sure to make that point to Aunt Catherine tomorrow," Richard said.

A companionable silence fell. *Perhaps now is the time to mention Georgiana.* The prospect made Richard's palms sweat. What if his cousin was opposed to their marriage? They had never discussed the possibility. Would he think Richard too old, too scarred by the war?

Would his position as a second son matter? Richard believed that Darcy would not care, but someone like Lord Robert certainly offered more prestige and connections.

Darcy rested his head against the back of his chair. "Now that Christmas is passed, I must decide what I am to do with Wickham. If I find he said anything to Lord Robert—"

"He told Lord Robert a tale, but the man did not believe it," Richard said.

Darcy let out a relieved breath. "Thank heavens." He frowned at the amber liquid in his glass. "Although the viscount did not seem quite so eager to speak with Georgiana at cards this evening."

"No. I believe he has given her up."

"Hmm," Darcy grunted, frowning. "Do you think Georgie is heartbroken?"

"No, I do not believe there was much affection on her part." This was a rather odd conversation to be having under these circumstances, but he was at a loss about directing the discourse as he required.

Darcy gave him a sidelong glance as if trying to discern what Richard knew. But then he finished the brandy in his glass and stood to pour himself some more from the decanter on the sideboard. "I cannot bear the prospect of paying any sum to Wickham," Darcy observed solemnly. "But if he spreads rumors about Georgiana long enough, someone will believe them."

A better opportunity would likely not present itself. Richard gulped a mouthful of brandy, hoping for some liquid courage. "I believe I may have an answer."

Darcy's eyes lit with interest as he seated himself again in the chair beside Richard's. "Indeed?"

Richard fixed his gaze on the crystal glass in his hands, turning it and watching the light sparkle off the different facets. "Yes...um...I do think that marriage might solve the problem..." This was more difficult than he had anticipated; sweat trickled down the back of his neck. "If she is married and the dowry is bestowed, Wickham can do little damage."

Darcy waved impatiently. "But you said Lord Robert will not make an offer. Surely you are not suggesting Worthy? That man is the worst kind of fool."

Richard licked suddenly dry lips. Why was this so difficult? "No, of course not. I—"

"She is not coming out for a whole year. Who do you think she should she marry then?" Darcy demanded.

"Well…" Richard gulped more brandy, which burned going down his throat. "Me, actually."

He chanced a glance over at his cousin, who was frozen with his glass halfway to his lips. *At least he did not laugh.*

"You?" Darcy finally echoed in a strangled voice.

"I…um"—Richard cleared his throat—"spoke with Georgiana this afternoon, and she gave her consent."

Darcy blinked rapidly. "She…" He set his glass down on a small table, leaning forward in his chair. "You do not need to do this, Richard. We will find some other way to stop Wickham. There is no need for you and Georgiana to make such a sacrifice."

Richard laughed. "It is no sacrifice, believe me."

His cousin frowned, and Richard realized his words could be misconstrued. "Darcy, I…have been in love with Georgiana for…a long time. I had never planned to say anything, but today…seeing her with that lord…I could not contain myself. I *had* to speak. I had only the slimmest hope she would return my affections—"

"You are her cousin. Of course she feels affection for you!"

Richard squeezed his glass more tightly. "Yes, er, I was concerned about that as well…right up until the moment she kissed me."

Darcy gaped. "She kissed you?"

"Yes." Richard could feel his cheeks heating. This was not a subject he would have chosen to share with his beloved's brother. "And not in a cousinly way, if you catch my meaning. She gave her consent, er, most enthusiastically."

Darcy said nothing. His expression showed only stunned blankness. Richard fought the need to stand and pace, preferably in a different room. *Have I said too much? Does he hate me? Will he withhold consent?*

"She…loves you?" Darcy finally asked.

"Yes. So she said."

"Why?" Darcy asked.

He said the first thing that came to mind. "Damned if I know." *Very well, perhaps that was not the most politic answer I could give.* "Elizabeth told Georgie to find someone who would love her as she is— without seeking to change her. She knows that I accept and love her eccentricities."

Darcy regarded him sharply. "Elizabeth said that?"

Richard nodded. "That is why Georgiana refused Lord Robert. He wanted her to cease her 'hoydenish' behavior."

"Then it is good she refused him!" Darcy declared, slapping his thigh.

"Yes, I thought so as well," Richard remarked dryly.

Darcy stared at his cousin for a moment and then laughed. "You are a sly one." He pointed at Richard. "I had no idea…"

The other man shrugged. "I could hardly declare myself to you when I did not know Georgiana's feelings."

Darcy stood abruptly and began pacing the room. "What about your commission?"

"I plan to sell it so I can remain in England."

"Where would you live?"

"We discussed this. Georgiana prefers to live in Derbyshire, so I thought to buy a small estate."

A ghost of a smile played on Darcy's lips. He would like to have his sister close to Pemberley. "Your parents will have no objection?" Darcy asked.

Darcy knew how difficult his parents could be. "I think they will be very pleased." Although they would no doubt have preferred that his older brother, Thomas, acquire one of the best dowries in England. Well, Thomas would have to settle for the earldom.

Darcy paced in silence for a minute, but Richard could practically hear furious thoughts churning through his brain.

Finally, Richard's anxiety overcame his patience. "Do I have your consent?"

Darcy stopped, focusing his intense gaze on Richard. "I will speak with Georgiana first, but then, yes, you do."

Richard blew out a breath. He had hoped Darcy would be amenable, but he had certainly dealt his cousin quite a shock. And shock often made people unpredictable. He stood and shook Darcy's hand. "Thank you for trusting me with her."

Darcy placed a hand on Richard's shoulder. "There is not a single soul in England I would feel more comfortable entrusting Georgiana's future to."

Richard's eyes burned, and he had to blink rapidly. "Thank you. Your trust means everything to me," he replied, trying not to think about secret visits into Pemberley's woods.

***

William had not been abed when Elizabeth arrived at their suite, even though she was retiring quite late. She thought the Christmas open house had gone well and hoped he was pleased with it. Still, their unwelcome guests lingered at Pemberley and showed no signs of departing before Twelfth Night—although perhaps Lydia would have burned the house down by then.

Elizabeth had screwed up her courage to speak with William about the problem but—uncharacteristically—he was not here. *Where could he be? Is he avoiding me?* Even thinking those questions made her chest ache.

But she was unwilling to surrender her plan altogether, so she had donned her dressing gown and ensconced herself in the sitting room which connected their bedchambers, reading a book to pass the time. When the clock chimed midnight and he was still not there, Elizabeth wondered if he planned to stay out all night. Would he sleep in his study—or a spare guest room? *What could it possibly mean?*

Finally, the door to the sitting room swung open, and William strolled in. He did a double take, noticing her in the chair. "You are still awake! Good!" He gave her a wide smile.

Oh no. He is foxed!

Yet he moved with perfect ease and grace to the chair next to hers. He demonstrated no clumsiness, and his eyes were not red. The quick kiss he gave her smelled faintly of brandy but not overwhelmingly so.

But what had happened to the cloud of gloom which had hung over husband the past few days?

He took her hand and gave it a squeeze. "I have the most marvelous news! Georgiana is betrothed!"

Her heart sank, but Elizabeth forced a smile. Over the past day she had concluded that the viscount was not the best choice for her sister-in-law, but opportunities to discuss it with Georgiana had eluded her. Now it was too late. "She accepted Lord Robert?"

William waved dismissively. "No, he is history; he could not hand Georgie's spirit, the coward. She has accepted an offer from Richard."

"Richard?" It was almost too good to believe.

"Yes, it seems that each has been nurturing a secret passion for the other, and Richard finally declared himself today. A Christmas engagement—quite romantic, is it not?"

Elizabeth jumped up from her seat and gave William an enthusiastic hug. "That is marvelous! Oh, William! I could not be happier."

"However, you do not appear surprised."

Elizabeth froze. Would he be displeased that she had not shared her suspicions with him? But his eyes twinkled, and a smile played about his lips. "I had come to…suspect a partiality existed, but only recently."

William leaned back in his chair. "I could not have asked for a better match for Georgiana. He suits her perfectly, and I know he can be trusted with her heart. Apparently we have you to thank for it."

"Me?" *But I never had a chance to speak with Georgiana!*

"You told Georgiana that she should wait for a man who loved her as she was, without seeking to change her—and she realized Richard was that man."

Elizabeth covered her mouth with her hand. "Oh my, I had no thought of my words being taken so seriously."

"It is excellent advice." He raised an eyebrow at her. "I wish someone had told *me* to accept my beloved the way she is. It would have saved me months' worth of grief." She smiled at him, a warm feeling radiating from her chest. "I shall announce their betrothal tomorrow at dinner. It will add quite a bit of merriment to the season."

"You seem very pleased about the match."

"I am. They are perfect for each other. And it may solve another problem."

She frowned. "What is that?"

William sighed heavily. "I did not wish to burden you with the story, but hopefully the marriage will help resolve it." He pinched the bridge of his nose. "Wickham threatened to spread a rumor that Georgiana was not…pure"—Elizabeth gasped—"if I did not give him her dowry."

"Her *dowry?*" Elizabeth cried.

"Yes, but now that Richard will get the dowry, I hope that Wickham will settle for a lesser sum. His threats have far less power if she is not to have a season in town."

"I hate the thought that you would give the scoundrel one penny."

William nodded his agreement. "Yes, but I doubt he will give up easily." He took a deep breath. "But we should speak of more pleasant things since today is Christmas—and we have cause for celebration." Then he raised his eyebrows and looked at her meaningfully. "Or perhaps we should not speak at all."

Elizabeth gave him a slow smile as he took her hand and tugged her into his lap. His arms cradled her gently as he kissed her quite thoroughly. When they were both out of breath, he gave her a shy look. "Will you please join me in my bed? I know this is not the Christmas we had planned, but we are alone at the moment. We should celebrate the holiday properly." Somehow his expression managed to be simultaneously abashed and lascivious.

"Indeed, the holiday must be properly celebrated," she said with mock solemnity.

Without any visible effort, William put one arm around her shoulders, another under her legs, and hoisted her into the air. Elizabeth gave a surprised squeak which made William chuckle. He carried her into his bedchamber and laid her reverently on the bed. When he did not immediately withdraw his arms, Elizabeth melted against him, enjoying the simple pleasure of his touch.

"I love you, William," she murmured.

"And I love you," he said, smiling. "But you are wearing too many clothes."

After that they did not communicate with words.

Chapter Fifteen

Thank heavens this is the last meeting with DuBois! Richard thought as he wended his way along the dirt track to the isolated pond. This was their fourth and final meeting. Richard had insisted that so many contacts put them unnecessarily at risk, but DuBois had claimed that he could not smuggle out all of the necessary papers at once. Richard suspected the man thought he could wrangle more money if they met more frequently.

Leaning against the lightning-struck tree, DuBois was waiting when Richard arrived.

"Do you have the papers?" Richard asked.

"Yes." DuBois gave a curt nod. "Do you have the money?" The man's French accent was so thick that Richard strained to understand him. "The money?" DuBois repeated impatiently.

Richard bit back a harsh retort. This transaction was about more than money, but that was all DuBois cared about. He pulled a purse of coins from his pocket and handed them to DuBois at the same moment the man gave him a sheaf of papers.

Richard examined the top pages to ensure they were the ones DuBois had promised. *Everything was in order. Thank goodness.* He felt some of the tension leave his body. DuBois counted his coins. "It is all there," Richard said testily.

DuBois gave an elaborate shrug. "I cannot be too careful. You might have miscounted."

There was a rustling in the undergrowth to Richard's right. He pulled out his pistol and turned, scanning the area. "Were you followed?" DuBois asked.

"No." Richard scowled. "Were you?"

When the noise was not repeated, Richard relaxed and lowered his gun. "Most likely it was just a deer or rabbit."

DuBois nodded as he shoved the coins into his pocket. "Still, we should not linger. We have both received what we came for."

"Indeed." Richard rolled up the papers and stuck them inside the front of his coat, pleased at the thought of never seeing the man again.

"I bid you adieu," DuBois murmured as he melted back into the forest.

"Goodbye."

Richard took another look at the copse of bushes that had produced the noise, but he saw nothing. As he strolled along the pathway to his horse, he wondered if he might be in time for luncheon with Georgiana.

***

Elizabeth awakened alone but took a moment to luxuriate in the knowledge that William was happy. Happy that Georgiana and Richard would marry. Happy that Elizabeth had played a small role in their betrothal. After all, when she had married, she had taken a vow to love and cherish William. When he was not happy, she felt she had failed.

Still, there was one obstacle to their lasting happiness. Or, rather, six obstacles in the form of six unwanted guests. Lying in bed, she pondered the predicament. Suddenly the answer came to her, so very obvious that she laughed aloud. "Yes, that will do very nicely." She sat up in bed and rang for the maid. She had a lot to do that day.

After she washed, dressed, and breakfasted, Elizabeth stole along the corridor to the house's kitchen wing. She had hoped to first consult William about her scheme but had seen no sign of him. However, he had given her authority over household matters, and this was most definitely a household matter. She quickened her pace, not wanting to miss the time when Pemberley's staff gathered to hear Mrs. Reynolds' instructions.

When she entered the room, the servants, sitting around a plain wooden table, hurried to their feet and gawked at her with round eyes. Elizabeth supposed that members of the Darcy family did not often venture into the kitchen. "Please be seated," she requested. They were a good staff, and she regretted that the volume of guests at Pemberley meant that so many of them had to work through the Christmas season. Yet another reason to dispense with their guests.

Once they had settled down, she questioned Mrs. Reynolds. "I need the assistance of the staff with a particular project. Would you mind if I addressed them?"

Mrs. Reynolds' eyebrows climbed, but she gave Elizabeth her motherly smile. "Of course, my dear."

She stood at the head of the table, twenty pairs of eyes upon her. The table behind Mrs. Reynolds was piled high with the boxes Elizabeth and Georgiana had assembled. None had been opened; the servants would take them when their work shifts ended. They did make an impressive display. Hopefully the servants would be pleased with their gifts.

"Pemberley is suffering from an excess of guests," Elizabeth started. A couple of maids giggled, and one of the footmen looked scandalized at this pronouncement. "Although you have all risen to this challenge admirably, the volume of guests has been an unexpected strain on our resources and my patience. So I have devised plans to encourage our guests to leave. However, I need your help. In particular, with encouraging Lady Catherine's departure."

She received some puzzled frowns, but more than a couple of servants appeared quite eager to help rid Pemberley of the scourge of Rosings Park.

"Begging your pardon, Mrs. Darcy, but how can *we* help?" Mrs. Reynolds asked.

Elizabeth took a deep breath. "My understanding is that Lady Catherine is a very demanding guest." The Pemberley staff was too polite to endorse this idea enthusiastically, but she saw a few nods. "I believe we have made her too…comfortable here at Pemberley. So as of today, our goal is to make her *less* comfortable. *Far* less comfortable."

Twenty pairs of eyes widened.

"If she says her bath water is not hot enough, tell her that is the warmest we can make it. If she wants you to cook the beef her way, offer her the chicken instead. If she asserts that her daughter is the best piano player in England, tell her that no, Miss Darcy must be." Several mouths hung open. One of the footmen chortled behind his hand. "Allow the fire in her chamber to go out. Make a mess of her hair. Serve her cold tea. Take a long time to summon her carriage. Complain about what an imposition her demands are for you. However, make it subtle enough that she does not suspect a conspiracy."

"But—but—" Rogers, one of the footmen, objected.

"I assure you that nobody will lose their position in the household because of this. In fact, I promise you all a bonus if she departs before Twelfth Night."

The servants looked at each other with a combination of excitement and consternation.

Elizabeth finally dared a look at Mrs. Reynolds. *Have I completely overstepped my bounds? Will she hate me for this scheme?* But the older woman's eyes were dancing. "Do you think you can do this?" Elizabeth asked the housekeeper.

"Yes, ma'am. After acceding to every one of that woman's demands, no matter how outrageous, it will be a delight to ensure she has an unpleasant experience at Pemberley."

"Good." Elizabeth exchanged a conspiratorial smile with the staff.

"Ma'am, forgive me," Rogers said. "Should we inform Mr. Giles of the plan?"

"Ah. Hmm..." Elizabeth considered. "I think not. He might find aspects of this plan... unpalatable."

"Or the whole thing," Rogers murmured with a grin.

"He will undoubtedly be happier if he can deny any knowledge," she concluded. She glanced around the table and noted nods of agreement; Giles did not appear to be universally liked. "Very good. I thank you all for your help."

The staff arose from the table and most dispersed to their various duties, although a few lingered about the kitchen. Mrs. Reynolds regarded Elizabeth expectantly. "Is there something else?" she asked the housekeeper.

Her lips were set in a thin white line. "Mr. Worthy has assembled some kind of experiment in the butler's pantry involving wheat and manure."

"Oh dear." Elizabeth's nose wrinkled as she imagined how the room must smell.

"Perhaps there is some way to hasten his departure?"

"I actually have a plan in the works," Elizabeth said. "Hopefully it will bear fruit."

The tension in the housekeeper's shoulders eased fractionally. "Very good."

Elizabeth turned to go, and then another thought occurred to her. "Mrs. Reynolds, I need to speak with Mr. Darcy. Do you know if he is in his study?"

The housekeeper's eyebrows rose. "Mr. Darcy left early this morning and said he would not return until suppertime." Her tone suggested surprise that Elizabeth was not already aware of his excursion.

He would be gone most of the day? How odd. Why had he not informed her? He always told her where he was going. Elizabeth's stomach, which had started to ease, began tying itself in knots once more. "Do you know where he went?"

The housekeeper frowned. "No. He went on horseback, though. He didn't take the carriage."

Behind Mrs. Reynolds, two of the scullery maids exchanged knowing glances. The back of Elizabeth's neck was warm, and her face heated. *Why should I be ashamed?* The staff might see this as a sign of the first cracks in her marriage, but she knew better. Did she not? Why did he not inform her where he was going?

As she hurried back to the main house, Elizabeth's elation over her plans began to flag. She believed he had forgiven her, that they had achieved a rapprochement the night before. And yet the day after Christmas, he apparently could not stand to be in the same house with her—even a house as big as Pemberley. Maybe he was simply trying to escape their plethora of guests, but then why conceal his destination?

She clamped her teeth together. *I will not cry. I have too many tasks to accomplish today.* She had wished to rid her home of unwanted guests by dinnertime. However, she could already feel her determination fading and lethargy sinking into her bones.

Perhaps I can finish the task tomorrow. But will it be too late by then? Will my marriage be over before it has barely started?

***

Bang! The pistol made a very satisfyingly loud noise as it kicked back into Georgiana's hand. She squinted at the target. Almost center but not quite. "You can do better," she muttered to herself.

She would have preferred to spend the morning with Richard, once again getting lost in the gardens. But upon awakening, she had discovered that he had gone for a ride, so she had decided to take advantage of the continuing mild weather and practice her shooting.

As she reloaded the gun, she heard her name being called in rather strident tones. Georgiana sighed. She need not look to know who approached.

"Hello, Aunt Catherine," she said as her ladyship, wrapped in many layers of capes, came into view. "How are you?"

Aunt Catherine pinched her lips together. "The damn fool maid left my window open! My room is approximately the same temperature as it is out here."

"That is unpleasant," Georgiana agreed.

The older woman walked carefully over the uneven ground and sat wearily on a nearby stone bench. "We should discuss the plans for your coming out. At the very least we should announce a date to ensure that no other young lady picks the same day."

Georgiana barely suppressed a shudder. She could think of few worse tortures than having Aunt Catherine plan her coming out. Fortunately, she would be spared that fate.

She took a deep breath, bracing herself for the coming storm. "I do not believe I will be having a come out."

She expected her aunt to be indignant, but instead she smiled broadly. "Have you accepted an offer? Tell me, which of the gentlemen did you choose? Either would be an excellent husband. Lord Robert would make a brilliant match. Mr. Worthy may not have a title, but—"

Georgiana finally brought herself to interrupt her aunt. "I did indeed accept an offer. But not from either of those gentlemen."

Aunt Catherine gaped, not surprisingly. She was probably wondering who Georgiana could have accepted an offer from in the past few days. "Not—? Then who—?"

"Richard," Georgiana said. Her aunt stared at her blankly. "Cousin Richard."

"Richard Fitzwilliam?" The older woman wrinkled her nose as if Georgiana had announced plans to run away with a gypsy caravan. "But he has no fortune!"

Georgiana fought to keep her composure. "I believe I have fortune enough for both of us."

"But, he is—well…"

Georgiana had rarely seen her aunt at such a loss for words. "He is a fine, upstanding man who will make a caring husband. And I love him."

Aunt Catherine waved love away impatiently. "He is a second son. It is not a bad idea to stay within the family, but you had much better marry Thomas; at least he will be earl one day."

If Georgiana did not find a distraction, she might tell her aunt what she actually thought. She turned her attention to her pistol, which was reloaded and ready to shoot. Sighting it along the target, she finally responded to her aunt. "I do not love Thomas, at least not that way."

"Bah!" Aunt Catherine exclaimed. "Marrying Richard is a fine match, but not a brilliant one." She snapped open her fan and applied it vigorously—a move surely intended for effect since it was not particularly warm. "Now, Lord Robert—"

How could their aunt dismiss Richard that way? He was the kindest, noblest man Georgiana knew. "Perhaps a brilliant match is not my goal," Georgiana said rather more forcefully than she intended. "I am far more interested in my happiness than impressing the *ton*."

Aunt Catherine shook her head as if Georgiana were a particularly difficult child—or a recalcitrant lapdog. "You Darcys are far too independent and stubborn. You can do better—"

He is her nephew! Georgiana could feel the pressure building up inside of her. She could bear any number of insults to her person, but slights to Richard could not be endured. How much more of this lecture could she take before she exploded at her aunt? Really, she needed to end this conversation. There had to be some way...

Aunt Catherine was still speaking. "...And the duty you owe your family—"

Georgiana could not take it anymore. She waved the pistol carelessly toward the woods and squeezed the trigger.

The pistol went off with a loud bang. Aunt Catherine startled, jumping in the air and dropping her fan.

"Oh dear!" Georgiana exclaimed, covering her mouth with her hand. "I quite wasted that shot; my attention was so distracted." She plucked the fan from the mud puddle in which it had fallen and returned it to her aunt, who took it gingerly between her thumb and forefinger.

Georgiana made a great show of hastily reloading the gun. "I promised myself to practice ten rounds today," she explained.

Aunt Catherine regarded the pistol warily. "Must it be so loud? Is there not a way to make it softer?"

Georgiana bit her lip as laughter threatened. "I am afraid not."

"Perhaps we should continue this conversation at another time," her aunt said in a rather strangled voice.

"That might be for the best." Georgiana did not look up from her task of reloading the gun until her ladyship had entered the house.

Chapter Sixteen

Richard could not have been happier. Georgiana had agreed to be his, and he was seated next to her at the table. Even now, their fingers were intertwined beneath the tablecloth and resting on his knee.

Most of the Pemberley party was assembled, although Mrs. Bennet's place was empty. They were dining in the breakfast room—which was a bit of a tight fit—as Lydia had ruined the dining table.

Darcy would make the betrothal announcement tonight, and then they would be allowed some handholding and kissing in public. Richard, for one, planned to make extensive use of the mistletoe.

Lord Robert, seated opposite them, did not appear to be enjoying his dinner. He glared at Richard and avoided looking at Georgiana. Perhaps he suspected their relationship was more than cousinly. Well, everyone would soon know.

"The maid was most impertinent!" Aunt Catherine complained loudly to Darcy. "She called me Lady Kate! You should turn her out without a reference!"

Elizabeth had concealed a laugh behind her napkin. "I shall have Mrs. Reynolds speak to Daisy about it," Darcy intoned solemnly, but there was a twitch of amusement on his lips.

"And I had your other maid shorten a pair of gloves for me," Aunt Catherine continued. "She returned them to me today. Well, the right one is a full two inches shorter than the left."

Darcy regarded his aunt. "Is that a problem?"

"Is it a problem?" Their aunt was practically shrieking by now. "I cannot wear a pair of gloves when one is so much shorter."

"Mrs. Reynolds will speak to Gwen about it. Perhaps she can make the other one shorter as well." How did Darcy keep a straight face when uttering such sentences?

"Shorten the other—?" their aunt spluttered. "What kind of a household are you running here?"

Darcy stiffened and gathered himself for a reply, but before he could say a word, there was a commotion outside the double doors. They swung open dramatically, hitting the walls.

Mrs. Bennet lurched into the room. "I am here!"

Elizabeth's face drained of color, and Mrs. Wickham rolled her eyes. Mr. Bennet hastened to his wife's side, taking her arm and speaking softly.

"No, I shall *not* return to my chamber," she replied loudly. "I have something to say, and I will say it—before you give me more of that powder to make me sleep!"

"Mrs. Bennet—"

But she was already stalking away. Standing behind her empty chair, she glared at a rather surprised Richard. *Why could she possibly wish to speak with me? I do not believe I have ever had a conversation with the lady.*

She pointed a finger at him. "I know what you are doing. I know everything!" she accused.

Richard could not guess what she was talking about. "Madam? I do not have the pleasure of understanding you."

"We were out for a walk this morning—patrolling for French scouts—when we saw you in the woods with that Frenchman!" Suddenly Richard recalled the rustling in the bushes. "You were exchanging money and papers. Lydia and I both saw it." Lydia nodded her head vigorously in confirmation.

Mrs. Bennet turned to Elizabeth. "I was correct that there are French spies right here in Derbyshire!" She gestured dramatically in his direction. "And the colonel is working with them!"

A stunned silence followed.

And broke immediately into a confusion of voices as everyone spoke at once.

"Silence!" Darcy bellowed. The table fell quiet. His gaze landed on Richard. "Do you have any idea what this is about?"

Unfortunately, he did. He had not expected to defend his actions from an accusation by Mrs. Bennet, of all people, but he did have an explanation prepared. "I did meet with a Frenchman in the Pemberley woods, but it was not for purposes of spying. He…I…owed him some money. That is all, nothing sinister." He hoped admitting to debts would divert attention. He tried to appear abashed by the revelation rather than angry at Mrs. Bennet's wild accusation.

Not surprisingly, Aunt Catherine was the first one to issue a condemnation. "Debts! Richard! What were you thinking? Neither a borrower nor a lender be." She lifted her chin so as to better convey her contempt.

Lord Robert regarded Richard with narrowed eyes. *Oh yes, the man is the local magistrate.*

"If it was nothing, then why did you meet in such an obscure location?" he asked.

Richard sighed. Perhaps admitting to other faults would throw off suspicion. "They were gambling debts." He very carefully did not meet Darcy's or Georgiana's eyes. Please God that the admission did not provoke Darcy to withdraw consent! "I did not want anyone to know."

The viscount shook his head, leaning forward on the table. "No, you could have easily met him in some isolated corner of Lambton. You went to great lengths to conceal your meeting. Why?" His gaze was piercing.

"I do not like it known that I indulge in gambling," Richard growled.

"This all seems very suspicious." Lord Robert rose from his seat, puffed up with importance.

Mr. Worthy's head bobbed up and down in agreement. "Most suspicious." This might be the first time he had heard the man render an opinion about something other than seed or fertilizer.

"La! Who knows what he was doing?" Lydia interjected. "It could be anything!"

"I am happy *someone* is taking it seriously!" Mrs. Bennet slid a meaningful look at her husband.

"A secret meeting with a Frenchman on Pemberley land...I am afraid I must detain you until we sort this matter out." The viscount's words suggested regret, but his eyes shone with a hint of delight.

"Detain him!" Georgiana cried, jumping to her feet. "Where?"

"Jail," Lord Robert said.

Darcy also shot to his feet. "Come now, is that not taking it a little far?" he cajoled Lord Robert. "Speaking with a Frenchman is not a crime."

"Speaking with one under mysterious circumstances could be," the viscount responded. "And I do not want the colonel to conveniently disappear while I am conducting this investigation." He glared balefully at Richard.

"Do not be ridiculous!" Lady Catherine pointed at Richard. "That is my nephew! He is a Fitzwilliam!"

"Be that as it may," Lord Robert said, "I must still secure him in the jail."

Darcy opened his mouth to object once again, but Richard waved him off. The more he protested, the guiltier he would appear. "Very well, take me to the jail. Then you can investigate and find out the truth of the matter. Mr. DuBois is staying at the Lambton Inn." And he would corroborate the story they had agreed upon.

"Richard, you cannot—" Georgiana had tears in her eyes.

Richard put his hand on hers, regretting that their betrothal announcement would be delayed. "It will be all right, Georgie. I have done nothing wrong. It will simply be a night in jail."

Lord Robert's gaze was intent on their clasped hands, suspecting their romantic relationship and hating Richard for it.

"Very well," Richard said to him. "Lead on."

***

The next morning the Darcy carriage halted before the Lambton jail. William shot Georgiana a look full of misgivings. At first he had refused to bring her, but Georgiana and Elizabeth together had worn down his resistance, arguing that she had the right accompany him.

As the driver helped Georgiana out of the carriage, she regarded the plain brick building with some apprehension. Jail was supposed to be a horrible and miserable place, and she knew it would be wretched to see the man she loved there. But if he could stand to be here, she could endure a visit of a few minutes—all that William would allow. She lifted her chin. *I will show Richard I can be brave.*

William put a sheltering arm around her shoulders as he opened the building's door and they stepped inside. The scent of unwashed bodies and refuse immediately overwhelmed her. It took all of her willpower not to recoil. While William spoke with the jailer, Georgiana scanned the small outer room. It was as dirty and grimy as she had expected, but it smelled even worse.

After giving them a suspicious and surly look, the keeper led them through a stout wooden door and down a narrow corridor to a cell at the back. There were four cells in total; three were occupied. In one, a dissolute man slept on the floor. In another, a man dressed in rags watched them with gaunt eyes and gave an alarmingly phlegmy cough as they passed by. Georgiana swallowed, fixing her eyes on the cell at the end of the corridor—Richard's cell.

The jailer opened the barred door and admitted them, apologizing for having to lock the door behind them. This cell was bigger than the other three and somewhat cleaner. As an earl's son, Richard was apparently entitled to the "luxury" accommodations. It was furnished with a cot and a table with a bowl and pitcher. The straw on the floor looked relatively fresh, but there was no denying the spider webs in the corners or the insects darting around the floor. The tiny barred window showed nothing but sky, and the room was only slightly warmer than the outside temperature.

Wearing his clothing from the previous night, Richard was worn and disheveled. His coat was stained in several locations, and his breeches had a rip near one knee. His hair could have been combed by a two-year-old. Georgiana had never seen such a welcome sight.

When they entered, Richard immediately sprang from the cot. "Why are you here?" he asked Georgiana. Without awaiting a response, he turned to William. "Why did you let her come?"

William bared his teeth in a tense smile. "I would like to see *you* forbid her."

"It is not his fault," Georgiana told Richard. "I threatened to mount my horse and come alone if he did not permit me to accompany him." Richard scowled, but Georgiana did not allow it to faze her. She had anticipated his displeasure. "My betrothed is in jail. This is where I belong."

Richard looked at William. "You cannot condone this madness."

William grinned at his cousin. "You cannot be more stubborn than a Darcy, Cuz. If it is truly a problem, then you should reconsider the betrothal."

Richard sighed and glanced away. "Best to make the visit brief then," he muttered.

Georgiana set a basket on the cell's crude wooden table. "Cook sent a sandwich and an apple, along with the last piece of gingerbread."

Richard did not make a move toward the basket but eyed it hungrily. "I thank you. It is a most welcome sight."

"I will speak to the viscount again," Darcy said. "Surely there is a way to have this ridiculous accusation dropped."

Richard sighed, shoving his fingers through his already disheveled hair. "That will prove difficult. The whole affair has become more…complicated since last night. They found DuBois dead."

"What?" William asked. Georgiana gasped.

Richard nodded. "Not far outside of Lambton. His throat was slit. Of course, I did not kill him, but—"

"Lord Robert will accuse you of it," William finished for him.

"He already has," Richard admitted. "He visited early this morning."

"Damnation!" William exclaimed.

"I would have no reason to kill DuBois; however, the viscount believes the debts alone are sufficient incentive. And, of course, he still suspects espionage."

William grimaced. "DuBois's death lends credence to that idea."

Richard nodded wearily. After only a night in this wretched place, he was already looking worn and haggard.

"At least tell us what happened," William demanded. "Then we can help."

"I told you," Richard said, his eyes sliding toward the barred window.

"You told us a fairy tale about paying gambling debts in the woods," Georgiana said. "Which I believe as readily as I believe you can fly to the moon. Tell us the truth."

Richard frowned. "That *is* the truth."

She folded her arms across her chest. "I neither believe you had gambling debts nor that you were so ashamed of them you had to have a secret meeting. Tell that story to someone who knows you less well than I."

Richard almost appeared…relieved? But he would not meet her eyes, keeping his gaze fixed on his hands. "Do you believe I am a spy?"

She snorted. "No."

The tension in his shoulders eased.

"I pray you honor us with the truth," William implored. "Perhaps we can assist you."

"We will hold whatever you say in confidence," Georgiana added.

Richard sighed, then scrutinized his fellow prisoners, who both appeared to be sleeping. He gestured the others to the far corner of the cell where he and Georgiana sat on the pathetic cot. William remained standing.

Richard lowered his voice. "I suppose secrecy does not matter as much now that DuBois is dead; however, you must hold my words in the strictest confidence." William and Georgiana nodded. "DuBois was a spy"—Georgiana gasped—"for the crown. The home office recruited him a year ago. He worked for a wealthy wool merchant from Belgium. A man on Napoleon's staff gathered intelligence and sent it to DuBois, who brought it here during his merchant's regular visits to Derbyshire.

DuBois's usual contact was not available this month, so my commanding officer, Major Blanchard, asked me to meet with the man. Since my family is here, my presence during the yule season would arouse no suspicions."

"Where are the papers he gave you?" William said. "They could prove your innocence."

Richard shook his head. "I already sent them in an express to Blanchard."

"There must be something we can do!" Georgiana cried.

Richard took her hand in his. "I have written to Blanchard and asked him to send someone with a letter to vouch for me. However, I do not know if the major remains in London. He may have gone home for Christmas."

"So tell Lord Robert the truth!"

Richard shook his head. "If I reveal one part of the network of spies, I could be putting other people at risk. I should not even be telling you, but I trust your discretion. Viscount Barrington is unlikely to believe me anyway."

"But this is awful, Richard!" Georgiana cried. "You could be in prison until Twelfth Night!"

He gave her a smile that did not reach his eyes. "I have been in worse positions, sweetling. I am not sleeping on hard ground, and I will not be sent into battle tomorrow." She shivered at the reminder of how dangerous his occupation could be.

In the ensuing silence, one of the other prisoners coughed again. What if Richard caught an illness here? The harsh conditions would make it more difficult for him to recover. An alarming number of prisoners died in jail.

"This is not acceptable!" Georgiana crossed her arms over her chest.

Richard laughed and kissed the back of her hand. "I appreciate your indignation on my behalf, but I will be fine." The strain around his eyes belied his words.

William shook his head. "I do not like it, Richard. You are too vulnerable here—unable to defend yourself. And I believe Lord Robert holds you responsible for Georgiana's refusal of his suit."

Georgiana's heart beat faster. Here was a danger she had not even considered.

Richard shrugged. "I can only await Blanchard's letter. There is nothing more I can do." He patted Georgiana's knee and smiled. "It will all work out. You shall see."

She nodded and mustered an encouraging grin.

The three cousins exchanged some more pleasantries after that. Too soon, however, the jailer marched into the cell and announced that visiting time was over.

Brother and sister exited the jail with a deep sense of dissatisfaction. "I wish there were more we could do," William remarked as they walked to the carriage.

Georgiana nodded, her lips pressed together. She had an idea for how to help Richard, but she could say nothing to William. He would never permit it.

Chapter Seventeen

Elizabeth awoke with steel in her spine.

She still did not know where William had gone the day before. He had returned shortly before dinner, a little weary and travel-stained but not obviously unhappy. When she had inquired —in passing—where he had gone, he had responded vaguely that he had "some things to attend to."

The answer had caused her heart to twist in her chest. He was keeping secrets from her, and that did not bode well for their marriage. The secret must have something to do with Elizabeth, or else he would have shared it with her. Had he simply wished to get away from Pemberley—and Elizabeth—for the day? Or was it worse? Was he considering removing to London and leaving her in the country?

She tried to shove away these unproductive thoughts. Regardless of the state of her marriage, she would see all of their uninvited guests gone by dinnertime, she vowed. It was the least she could do for the sake of her marriage—and her sanity.

Her mother had accused Colonel Fitzwilliam of treason. Her sister had nearly burned down Pemberley—twice! Lydia's husband had threatened Georgiana's reputation. Lord Robert had arrested Georgiana's betrothed. Mr. Worthy was creating unique odors in the butler's pantry. Lady Catherine had thrown the staff into a state of panic.

And they still did not have any marmalade!

It was time to put her plans into action.

Her task was to have Lord Robert's clothing packed and sent to the Barrington estate. Given that the viscount had arrested William's cousin, she did not think she was taking excessive liberties nor did she imagine the lord would wish to linger under their roof.

Her mother and father were breakfasting, having risen later than the rest of the household. Elizabeth seated herself at the table, pasting on a smile as they exchanged greetings. Contemplating the best approach, Elizabeth watched her mother chew over her toast and listened to her complaints about the quality of ham at Pemberley.

Finally, she said, "Mama, I know you are concerned about the safety of the neighborhood, particularly now that we know a Frenchman has been here."

Elizabeth's father shot her an alarmed look which asked why she was volunteering for this conversation. She returned a serene smile.

Mrs. Bennet stopped in mid-chew and then spoke around a mouthful of toast. "I had hoped Mr. Darcy could get the militia to guard Pemberley. Lydia's husband could help."

Elizabeth hid a wince. William would sooner let *Napoleon* guard Pemberley. "Actually I was concerned that Derbyshire is not safe enough."

Mr. Bennet cleared his throat loudly, but Elizabeth ignored him. Leaning forward, she caught her mother's eyes. "Perhaps you and Papa should go further north—a greater distance from France."

Her mother's eyes lit with excitement. "Yes, that is what I have been saying to Mr. Bennet this past fortnight. Did you have somewhere in mind?"

The fish had taken the bait; time to reel it in. "Actually I do. Mr. Darcy has a property in Scotland. I wrote to the housekeeper to make it ready for visitors. You could be there in three or four days—in time for Twelfth Night."

"Scotland!" Mrs. Bennet's eyes grew round. Her husband's mouth gaped.

Elizabeth smiled at her mother, but her eyes were on her father. "I know Papa has always wanted to see the highlands."

Her father's expression had evolved from panicked to pleased. "That is true," he said, leaning back in his chair. "A trip to Scotland sounds very…restful."

"You should come with us!" her mother exclaimed. "And Lydia and her husband. I want you all to be safe. Perhaps we should send for Kitty and Mary and Jane."

Elizabeth smiled, touched that her mother cared about them—in her own bizarre fashion. "I cannot go now. William has duties here, as does Mr. Wickham. But perhaps we can join you for a visit in a few months."

"A few months?" her father repeated. "How long can we possibly stay?"

"As long as you would like," Elizabeth said. "You might want to travel around a bit, see the countryside." Her father's smile grew broader by the second. "Think of it as a holiday."

"But it is not, of course." Her mother shoved some eggs into her mouth as she spoke. "We are ensuring our safety."

Elizabeth nodded solemnly. "Of course." She waited until her mother had swallowed. "So this would be an acceptable solution for you?"

Mrs. Bennet beamed. "Yes, indeed. The French will never find us in Scotland. What is his property like?"

"I have never seen it, but I understand that it is a bit like a castle."

Her mother clapped her hands together. "A castle! How marvelous."

"That sounds lovely, my dear," her father said.

Elizabeth did not allow her relief to show, but inside she was celebrating. "We can have the carriage ready by noon."

"Oh, I do not know if we can be prepared to leave today," her mother said dubiously.

However, Elizabeth was prepared for this objection. "William is concerned about the prospect of snow, and now that we know there are Frenchmen in Lambton..."

Her mother surged to her feet, overturning a cup of coffee in the process. "There is no time to waste. Mr. Bennet, come along!"

Her father narrowed his eyes at the summons but stood to escort his wife from the room.

"The servants will help you pack," Elizabeth added.

Mrs. Bennet hurried from the room, murmuring about "Scotland" and "castles." Her father's eyes twinkled as he regarded Elizabeth. "Thank you, my dear."

"You are very welcome, Papa."

He kissed her on the top of the head and strode away.

One problem solved. Many more yet to go.

***

Darcy was writing a strongly worded letter to Major Blanchard in the hopes of pushing the army officer into action. He had also secured for his cousin the best lawyer in Derbyshire, but the man could do little without any kind of exculpatory evidence. As he wrote, Darcy pondered what else he could possibly do to help Richard.

There was a timid knock at his study door. "Enter," he called absently without looking up from his letter.

When he did notice who entered, he was forced to do a double take. "Mrs. Annesley?"

Georgiana's companion had been ill for several weeks and had only lately returned to her duties. As a result, she had not been visible at Pemberley in recent days. She looked more than ill today, however. Her face was several shades too pale, and she was wringing her hands incessantly.

"What is the matter?" he asked as she sank into the chair opposite him.

She patted her hair, a nervous habit. "I-I was s-seeking out Miss Darcy and c-could not find her anywhere. Then I found this note on her dressing table."

Darcy's heart started beating wildly when she handed him a paper. This could not possibly bode well. He perused the short note, written in Georgiana's unmistakably neat handwriting, and threw it down on the desk. Closing his eyes, he suppressed a very ungentlemanly impulse to curse in front of a lady. His second impulse was to shout at the companion—which would be equally unproductive as well as unfair. Georgiana was an almost grown woman who barely needed a companion anymore. Mrs. Annesley could not be expected to contain every wild impulse.

After a moment he had gained enough control to speak. "When did she write this?"

Mrs. Annesley pulled her shawl more tightly around herself. "I-I did not seek her for quite a while. It must be s-several hours ago now."

Darcy ground his teeth. "No hope of catching her then."

"I am so sorry, Mr. Darcy. I will tender my resignation—"

"It is not your fault," he said.

She gave a bitter laugh. "I beg your pardon, sir, but it is no one's fault but mine. At this moment my charge is riding to Matlock—alone! That is precisely the kind of mischance it is my job to prevent."

"You have been sick. And no one could have prevented this—not when Georgiana is determined to do something. She is stubborn and clever. If she had been inclined toward mischief earlier in her life, neither you nor I could have prevented it. We are fortunate she exercises good judgment—usually." Darcy suddenly had a great deal more sympathy for Lydia Bennet's father.

"Sir, I insist. I must—"

"I will not accept your resignation!" he thundered.

Mrs. Annesley paled even further, and Darcy instantly regretted his words. He never yelled at the staff, no matter the circumstances. "I apologize for my raised voice, Mrs. Annesley. I am…anxious about Georgiana."

The older woman nodded mutely.

He ran both hands through his hair. "At the moment I must focus my resources on ensuring Georgiana's safety. We will discuss your employment status later."

Mrs. Annesley clasped her hands in her lap. "I have comforted myself with the thought that she is an excellent rider."

Darcy nodded absently, thinking that her horsemanship skills were the least of his worries. The roads in Derbyshire were generally safe, but crime could occur anywhere. At least if she wore her split skirt, the ride would be easier and faster. *Damn it! Why could she not tell me of her plan? I could have helped—or prevented it.*

He crumpled the note in his fist. It did not explain *why* she was riding to Matlock, although he did not doubt it had something to do with Richard's incarceration. Most likely she hoped to get Richard's father, the earl, to intervene. But Lord Robert was a viscount; he would not yield easily to pressure, even from another peer. Darcy feared her trip was in vain.

He pulled out a fresh piece of paper. His first thought had been to ride after her, but he would arrive at Matlock long after she did. However, he could have a message delivered to his aunt and uncle's house, Edgemont Manor, about her ride.

But what would he do if she did not arrive?

Chapter Eighteen

Mr. Wickham's eyes widened when he saw who awaited him in the parlor of the Lambton Inn. "Elizabeth! Are you alone?"

"Mrs. Darcy to you. And yes," she said stiffly.

A brief frown drifted over his face only to be replaced with his habitual smirk. She might have taken him unawares, but he would not show it. He slouched into the chair opposite hers. "Unseasonably warm weather, wouldn't you say?"

Elizabeth was in no mood to discuss pleasantries. "I came to discuss Georgiana's future," she said tersely.

He gave her a lazy smile. "I suppose your husband has told you about—"

"Your blackmail attempt? Indeed. But I am here to inform you about circumstances which have only developed recently."

"Do tell." His eyebrows rose, but his smarmy smile remained unchanged.

"Colonel Fitzwilliam was arrested for meeting with a Frenchman yesterday."

A corner of Mr. Wickham's mouth curled up. "Lydia visited this morning and gave me that news. Could not have happened to a nicer fellow."

Elizabeth took a deep breath. This was where she needed to play her part most convincingly. "Lydia did *not* know then that the Frenchman is dead—slit across the throat."

Mr. Wickham's eyes widened as he drew the same conclusion the magistrate had. Then he very consciously resumed a pose of affected unconcern, staring at his nails. "This is nothing to me. I did not know the Frenchman and do not care about the colonel." His voice had a good approximation of his earlier lazy drawl.

Elizabeth bared her teeth in a smile. "The colonel is newly engaged to Miss Darcy."

Now the man blanched.

Nonchalantly, Elizabeth examined a small irregularity in the stitching of her glove. "Naturally he is aware of your threats against Miss Darcy's reputation—and her *dowry*." Mr. Wickham flinched at the word. "No doubt the colonel will be freed from jail soon." She wished she were as confident of that eventuality as she sounded. "And he will not be pleased by your behavior."

Having leapt from his chair, Mr. Wickham retreated from Elizabeth as if *she* were the threat.

"I thought to warn you. I do not care for *your* sake." She flicked imaginary dust from her skirt. "But Lydia would be unhappy if you were hurt."

Mr. Wickham rubbed his jaw with a trembling hand. "P-perhaps it would be best if we were gone from Derbyshire when he is released."

"That might be wise," Elizabeth said.

The man already had one hand on the doorknob. "And please tell him that my 'little joke' with Darcy was just an amusement, not a serious threat."

"So you disavow any further plans to damage Georgiana's reputation or lay claim to her dowry?" Elizabeth asked.

Mr. Wickham waved his hands in a dismissive gesture. "Yes, yes! Of course. It was just a lark! I would never do anything to hurt G-the colonel's fiancée. I will return north and forget all about it."

"I am sure the colonel will be pleased to hear it." She rose and strolled to the door as well. "He may be getting out of jail as early as today," she said. "So you might want to hasten your departure."

The man's eyebrows rose again. "Yes, yes. Of course. When you return to Pemberley, please ask Lydia to prepare for travel."

"I shall," Elizabeth said with a smile.

Another problem solved.

***

Georgiana had never been so grateful for a fast horse. But then she had never ridden with a man's life—or at least his freedom—at stake. True to her bloodlines, Athena's gait was smooth and sure, and she covered the miles swiftly.

Even so, by the time Edgemont, the seat of the Earl of Matlock, came into view, Georgiana's energy was flagging. Athena fared little better; she was not accustomed to running such long distances.

As the house loomed larger and larger, Georgiana's anxiety increased. The trip had seemed like a splendid idea back at Pemberley—the only way to clear Richard's name and rescue him from that wretched jail. But now...did she really have the temerity to ask for this favor?

She was only a girl of nearly eighteen years—one who appeared rather rumpled and travel-worn at this moment. In addition, she was wearing her divided skirt. *What will they think? What if they laugh at me or ignore me?* Her whole body heated in anticipation of that humiliation, and the impulse to turn around was strong. It was not too late. William would not have spread the news. No one would know of her misadventure, save William, Mrs. Annesley, and possibly Elizabeth.

Then Georgiana conjured up the image of Richard sitting in the dingy cell. Potential mortification was nothing compared to what he was enduring. She straightened in the saddle. Elizabeth would not be deterred in the same situation. Nor would William. *I am a Darcy. I can do this.*

She reined in her horse at Edgemont's front portico. A groom raced into the driveway to take Athena's reins. "Miss Darcy!" he exclaimed. "We weren't expecting you."

"I daresay not," she replied, sliding down from the saddle.

After lingering to discuss the horse's care, she hurried toward the house. Edgemont's front entrance was far grander than Pemberley's, with an enormous mass of stone carvings surrounding the doorway. It was designed to be intimidating, and Georgiana had often felt the weight of its wealth and grandeur as a child. Today Georgiana lifted her chin a little higher and slowed her steps to a dignified pace. No one must guess she had any misgivings.

The butler opened the door, welcomed her, and took her cloak. Her aunt hastened in from the saloon just as Georgiana strode into the elegant front hall, bedecked with elaborate gilt décor.

"Georgiana!" Aunt Susan hurried across the marble floor. "I just learned of your arrival." She embraced her niece enthusiastically. "Where are the others? Is everyone well at Pemberley?"

"Everyone else remains at Pemberley." Georgiana resisted the temptation to let the words spill out. "And everyone is well, for the most part. However, I have a story to tell and a favor to ask."

Aunt Susan took both of Georgiana's hands with a worried frown. Some of Georgiana's anxiety must have been communicated to her. "Anything you need, my dear. Of course."

She swallowed hard; this was the moment of truth. "The favor is not from you and Uncle Hugh. I need to beg a favor of General Burke."

Aunt Susan gaped as if Georgiana had lost her mind. "General Burke?"

The force of her aunt's shock made Georgiana want to shrink into herself, but she threw back her shoulders. This was for Richard's sake. She could endure far more if necessary. "Yes. It is most urgent."

Her aunt's eyes widened in alarm, but she gestured toward the saloon. "He and his wife are taking tea with us."

Georgiana nodded, took a deep breath, and strolled into the room directly behind the entrance hall, trying to project a confidence she did not experience. It was a large, elegant room, oval in shape, with three groupings of furniture which guests could use for gatherings and conversation. Her uncle was seated with a man and woman Georgiana did not recognize. General Burke was tall and broad, with a bushy mustache and fierce eyes. Of course, he was not wearing a uniform, but she had no difficulty picturing him shouting orders on a battlefield.

After exchanging curtsies and bows, her uncle invited Georgiana to sit and have some tea. She accepted a cup, but the urgency of her message precluded taking more than a sip. "Georgiana said she needed to speak with you, Henry," Aunt Susan said in a tone that suggested a dog had just sung a Christmas song.

"Me?" The general's formidable gaze fell on Georgiana, and she knew her face was heating. "What is your business with me?" His tone was gruff.

"It is about my cousin, Colonel Richard Fitzwilliam." Now she had the focused attention of everyone in the room. "He is in jail in Lambton."

Aunt Susan gasped; for a moment it appeared that she might be in need of her smelling salts. "W-when did this occur?"

"Whatever for?" Uncle Hugh asked. Despite his outward composure, his teacup rattled so loudly that he was swiftly forced to set it down.

"Who would imprison the colonel?" the general's wife asked.

General Burke waved for silence. "Let the girl tell her story."

"He had been seen meeting with a Frenchman, a Mr. DuBois, in the woods at Pemberley and was accused of being a spy."

Aunt Susan gasped again and covered her mouth with her handkerchief.

Georgiana forged on. "You know he is not a spy." She focused intently on the general. "He was following Major Blanchard's orders."

She paused for a moment. Finally, the general nodded. Georgiana's shoulders relaxed a fraction. There was a chance the general had been unaware of Richard's orders.

"The magistrate threw Colonel Fitzwilliam into jail," she explained. "He has written to Major Blanchard in London, but it could take him a week or more to respond. Richard cannot reveal the truth without risking the secrecy of his mission."

Aunt Susan now regarded the general with anxious eyes. He rubbed his chin, his expression solemn. "This is a most disturbing chain of events."

She had almost forgotten the most important part! "Oh, and they found Mr. DuBois dead this morning on the outskirts of Lambton, so now the magistrate thinks Richard murdered him."

Aunt Susan emitted a little shriek; her husband put a comforting arm around her shoulders.

The general's eyes narrowed. "DuBois is dead?"

Georgiana nodded, secretly relieved at his visible alarm. Her worst fear had been that he would deny knowledge of Richard's actions.

She took a deep breath. "Would you be willing to write the magistrate and attest to Colonel Fitzwilliam's innocence?" she asked.

He was still rubbing his chin. "No."

Georgiana's chest constricted. What would she do now?

General Burke continued, "I am not sure that buffoon of a magistrate would credit a letter. I am afraid I must go to Lambton in person."

Relief flooded Georgiana's body so swiftly that she feared she might faint.

"Capital idea! I shall take you there in my coach!" Uncle Hugh remarked.

The general smiled. "That would be much appreciated. I have spent a lot of time on horseback recently."

"I am going as well," Aunt Susan announced. "No one is rescuing my son from jail without me!" She gave Georgiana a sharp look. "Would you like to rest here, or do you wish to accompany us?"

Georgiana was exhausted, but the choice was easy. "I am going with you."

Chapter Nineteen

The sound of Lady Catherine's shrieks was music to Elizabeth's ears. She happened to be standing in the marble hall when her ladyship stormed down the stairs. Oddly, Giles seemed to be following her. The older woman shook her finger at Elizabeth. "I have instructed my maid to pack my trunk, and my footmen are readying the carriage. I will not be persuaded to spend one more day under this roof."

"Very well," Elizabeth said.

"Not one more day!" she repeated but then fell silent when she realized Elizabeth did not object.

In truth Elizabeth was struggling to prevent her elation from showing on her face. "I am sure you will be very comfortable at Rosings. It is always pleasant to spend Twelfth Night in one's own home."

Lady Catherine drew herself to her full height. "Do you not want to know why I am departing?"

"I have no objection to your telling me," Elizabeth replied.

The other woman sniffed at this answer, but recognizing it was the best response she would get, she embarked on her rant. "It is your staff! The level of mismanagement—! Well, you should just fire the lot of them and start over."

"I am sorry you had an unpleasant experience with them," Elizabeth said with as much sincerity as she could muster.

"I discovered a fly in my tea! A fly! My luncheon was barely edible. I sent a stocking for mending, and your girl says she lost it! How could she lose it? And worst of all"—her voice quivered with indignation—"they are all referring to me as Lady Kate!"

Elizabeth bit her lip so a stray chuckle would not escape.

"One of the footmen even called me *Lady Katie!*" She peered down her nose at Elizabeth. Behind her ladyship, Giles regarded her with an even haughtier expression. "What do you say to that?"

Elizabeth shrugged. "It is so hard to get good help."

Lady Catherine stared at her incredulously for a moment. "Well, I am not accustomed to such treatment, I tell you! It will be a long time before I darken Pemberley's doorstep again!"

"This is a heavy burden indeed, but we will bear it as best we can."

The other woman glared at Elizabeth. "Your only servant who is worth anything is Giles." She gestured to the butler. "And I have resolved to take him with me."

Elizabeth's eyebrows rose.

"I am tendering my resignation," Giles said with the scantest courtesy.

Well, this will make life at Pemberley easier. "Very well. Would you like me to have a maid pack your things?"

Giles appeared a bit crestfallen that she had not begged him to stay. "No. I have already attended to that," he informed her frostily.

"I hope you enjoy Kent," Elizabeth said to him. Then she directed her attention to Lady Catherine. "I would remind you that he has been supervising the staff you found so lacking." Giles paled, and Lady Catherine spluttered. "But perhaps the staff at Rosings Park will be less unruly."

"I am taking my leave immediately." Lady Catherine swept her way toward the door with Giles trailing behind. "I give no regards to you, your husband, or your parents!" With that declaration, Lady Catherine strode out of Pemberley's main entrance, refusing to close the door behind her.

Elizabeth stepped up to the open doorway to watch Lady Catherine and Giles stalk down the pathway to her waiting carriage. A moment later she noticed Mrs. Reynolds standing at her elbow with a slight smile on her face. "So that finally did it," the housekeeper said. "I cannot say I shall miss Giles."

"Nor will I." Elizabeth glanced sidelong at the older woman. "I do have one question, though."

"Hmm?"

"Where on earth did you find a fly in December?"

***

The food was awful, the cell was cold, and the vermin were plentiful, but the worst part of jail, Richard decided, was the boredom. The life of a soldier could often be unpleasant, but at least it was usually full of activity and meaning. Spending his day lying on a cot with nothing to occupy him but his thoughts—that had nothing to recommend it.

The sun had already gone down, but Richard estimated it to be only around dinnertime. He had lit the cell's two candles, but they did little to dispel the pervasive gloom. Not for the first time, he wished for his watch, but it would have been a target of theft.

Suddenly the stillness of the evening was interrupted by the sounds of people entering the building. Who would be arriving at this hour? The jailer had made it clear that he would not tolerate visitors after three o'clock. Did they have a new prisoner? Richard lifted himself from the cot and covered the distance to the cell's door in three strides. The other two prisoners also stood by their cell doors awaiting a chance to glimpse the visitors.

The door to the cell block opened to reveal the most unlikely parade of people. The jailer—with a very surly expression—then General Burke, then Richard's mother and father, followed by Darcy and Georgiana. Lord Robert, the magistrate, a disgruntled scowl permanently affixed to his face, brought up the rear of the procession. *What in the world?* Not only was Richard mystified how this particular collection of people had come to be here, he could not understand *why*.

The jailer opened the door to Richard's cell, and people poured in. His attempt to salute the general was interrupted when his mother pulled him into an embarrassingly effusive hug.

Richard finally disentangled himself from his mother and spent a long moment staring at Georgiana, wishing he could kiss her. "What has come to pass?" Richard's gaze jumped from face to face but finally settled on the general, as the person he least expected to see.

"We just paid a visit to that *magistrate.*" The scathing look General Burke directed toward Lord Robert left no doubt of his opinion of the man's character. The viscount bristled but remained silent. "I explained that you were an army officer carrying out a clandestine assignment for the crown and certainly had nothing to do with DuBois's death."

"Which the magistrate should have known," Darcy interjected, "since he and you were both at Pemberley when the man perished."

Even in the inadequate light, Richard could perceive Lord Robert's deep flush.

"He agreed to release you," explained Richard's father. "We decided to accompany him and lend our assistance." *How much help could possibly be necessary?* Richard rather suspected that they thought he might need protection.

The cell was large as these things go, but it was quite crowded under the circumstances—even with the magistrate and the jailer remaining in the corridor. Richard was eager to leave the premises, but one question still nagged him. He searched the smiling faces. "How did you even hear of my predicament?" he asked General Burke.

When the general did not respond immediately, Richard looked inquiringly at William. But his cousin's gaze was fixed on Georgiana—as were all the others in the room. Meanwhile, his fiancée had turned bright pink. Nevertheless, she lifted her chin. "I rode up to Matlock to ask for the general's help."

"You did a three-hour ride in the winter? Alone?" Richard asked incredulously. Thank God he had not known—and could see she was unharmed.

"That is what *I* said." Darcy threw up his hands in exasperation.

"You were in *prison!*" Scowling at Richard, she folded her arms across her chest. "I was not about to remain snug and warm at Pemberley while you languished here!"

"You could have sent a note!" Richard exclaimed.

She tilted her head and regarded him with narrowed eyes. "I could have sent a note to a general I had never met with details of a secret government mission I was supposed to know nothing about?"

Richard's father chuckled. "She has a point." Richard glared at his father for this treachery.

"We can argue about this later," his mother said. "I would like to depart this filthy place and take Richard somewhere clean and warm."

"Amen," said his father.

And that was how Colonel Richard Fitzwilliam was released from prison in time for Twelfth Night.

Chapter Twenty

"Would you like some tea, Mr. Worthy?" Elizabeth inquired.

The gentleman in question seemed a bit flustered by such a simple question. "Er...that is...yes. I thank you." He searched the drawing room once more with his eyes. "Are we the only ones partaking of tea?"

She poured him a cup. "Indeed. Mr. and Miss Darcy are fetching Colonel Fitzwilliam from jail. Everyone else seems to have departed for good, and here I expected them to stay through Twelfth Night."

Mr. Worthy seemed even more disconcerted by this news; it was a bit awkward being the sole remaining guest, particularly since he was not related to the family. But Elizabeth suspected his anxiety had more to do with the other two occupants of the drawing room. Miss Olivia Bracknell and her mother, Mrs. Gloria Bracknell, had arrived at Pemberley at Elizabeth's express invitation.

Miss Bracknell regarded Mr. Worthy with an intensity that he apparently found unnerving; his eyes remained fixed on his tea cup, which could not possibly be that interesting. Finally, words burst from the young lady at a rapid pace. "Are you the John Worthy who published the article on crop rotation in the *Derbyshire Agricultural Quarterly*?"

Mr. Worthy raised his eyes to hers before replying. "I am. Did you read my article?"

"Yes!" Miss Bracknell watched him with shining eyes. "But do you think the technique would be as effective for potatoes—or is it mainly for grain crops?"

Mr. Worthy blinked several times and settled back into his chair. As he launched into a lengthy disquisition on grains and crop rotation, Miss Bracknell hung on his every word, oblivious to anyone else in the room. Mrs. Bracknell regarded Elizabeth over their heads with a small, satisfied smile and a tiny nod.

Half an hour later, Mr. Worthy was preening over an invitation to dine at the Bracknells' nearby estate and stay the night since it would be too late to travel back to Pemberley. Miss Bracknell was beside herself with joy at having such an agricultural luminary come to their house. The couple chattered with great animation as they strolled through the marble hall toward the Bracknells' carriage.

Mrs. Bracknell hung back a moment to speak with Elizabeth. "I do not know where you found this young man, but he is...perfect!" Her smile could not have been any wider.

At a visit a few weeks ago, Mrs. Bracknell had lamented to Elizabeth about her daughter's unusual interest in the agricultural operations of their estate and fretted that she would never find a husband who would suit her unique character.

Tears of joy sparkled on the woman's eyelashes. "I cannot express my appreciation enough, Mrs. Darcy."

Elizabeth laughed. "They are not wed yet."

"I would wager they will be by Twelfth Night." Mrs. Bracknell winked.

"I would not bet against that," Elizabeth laughed.

The woman gave Elizabeth's hand a squeeze and then followed the others into the dark winter night.

Elizabeth closed the door behind them with a particular sense of accomplishment.

**

Sitting in the back of his coach with a reunited Richard and Georgiana, Darcy felt distinctly superfluous. Occupying the bench seat across from him, they had eyes for no one but each other as they murmured in low tones.

After Georgiana and the Matlock party had arrived at Pemberley, there had been a great deal of debate and strategizing. Finally, they had decided on a plan that involved taking two carriages to the Barrington family estate to convince Lord Robert to release Richard. Then had come the journey to the jail.

It had been several hours since Darcy left Pemberley, although it felt like an eternity. He could only hope that once he returned home, their various guests would be somewhat restrained or—dare he hope—retired for the night. He was not certain how he would cope with another conversation about a French invasion or Aunt Catherine's dictates about how to conduct his life.

In the morning he would be required to manage the headache known as Wickham. The thought almost made him groan aloud. Darcy did not know how the man would react to word of Georgiana's betrothal. Would it discourage him, or would his demands persist? Darcy should formulate a plan for each contingency, but his exhausted brain did not want to consider the subject.

Finally, the carriage jiggled to a halt, and the footman opened the door. They dragged themselves through the front entrance to be greeted with a welcoming smile from Elizabeth that nearly wiped away Darcy's exhaustion. He gave her a quick kiss, and then she hugged Richard.

"I am so please you are out of that terrible place," she declared.

"As am I," Richard said fervently.

"Did anyone from Matlock accompany you here?" she asked Darcy.

"No, they all returned to Edgemont."

"Just as well," Georgiana opined tartly. "We have a surfeit of guests as it is." Richard grinned as he put his arm around her and pulled her toward him.

Darcy was about to admonish his sister for her manners—what if one of their guests heard? But then he noticed Elizabeth harboring a secretive smile. "Not anymore," she announced to the others.

They were all gone? Surely that was too much to hope for. Darcy's brows knit together. "What do you mean?"

"My parents left this morning, and Lydia and Wickham in the afternoon. Your aunt stormed out before tea while Mr. Worthy departed immediately after. And I ate dinner all by myself!"

Darcy took both of Elizabeth's hands in his. "You can work miracles! How did you accomplish it?"

She laughed. "I simply gave each guest something they greatly desired. My parents have an opportunity to visit Scotland. Mr. Worthy met a nice young lady who likes agriculture. And your aunt has an unending source of complaints for at least the next year—and a new butler."

Darcy arched an eyebrow. "Giles is gone to Rosings?" Elizabeth nodded, watching him with a furrowed brow. "Thank God!" Elizabeth gave a relieved laugh. "I did not have the heart to dismiss the man since he served my father, but he really had grown quite insufferable."

"Oh, William!" Georgiana exclaimed. "Now that he is gone, can we redecorate this room?" She gestured to the cold, uncompromising grandeur of the marble hall. "Elizabeth and I would like an entrance that is more welcoming, but Giles would have complained endlessly."

Elizabeth nodded eagerly.

"Certainly," Darcy said. "I would not mind if the room had a warmer sensibility." Then he frowned. "And, Elizabeth, what about the Wickhams?"

"They are simply grateful to escape Derbyshire alive." Darcy gaped at her, and she laughed. "I will tell you the whole story over breakfast tomorrow."

Richard grinned broadly. "Darcy, I can indeed see the value of a clever wife."

"Yes, you have dispatched with our guests quite admirably," Darcy told her. Elizabeth beamed at the compliment. "However, this somewhat detracts from my Christmas surprise to you," Darcy said with a trace of chagrin.

"Christmas surprise?" Now it was Elizabeth's turn to gape. "I-I w-was not expecting anything, William!"

He laughed. "Hence the word 'surprise!'"

Now her eyes were suspiciously shiny. "What is it then?"

He looped his hands around her waist. "I spent much of yesterday seeking out a suitable cottage on the shores of Rudyard Lake…so that we would have a peaceful place to ourselves for Twelfth Night since our house was so overrun with visitors."

"So that is where you went! I thought—" She quickly covered her mouth with her hand.

"You thought what?"

She hesitated but then leaned forward until their foreheads were touching. "I thought you were angry at me about the plethora of guests and their ill behavior."

He put both of his hands on the sides of her face. "Angry with you? Never, my darling. Never." Then he kissed her in a way that demonstrated precisely how not-angry he was.

Richard ostentatiously cleared his throat. "We are still in the room, you know. You should reserve such behavior for the bedchamber."

"Richard!" Georgiana laughed. "The things you say!"

After releasing his wife, Darcy eyed his cousin with an attempt at menace, but he could not help laughing. Richard returned a teasing smile.

But then his cousin's expression grew more solemn. "I could take Georgiana to Edgemont if you and Elizabeth would like some privacy for the remainder of the Christmas season."

Darcy caught Elizabeth's eye, but she gave a slight shake of her head. "No," Darcy responded. "You and Georgiana are the people we would most wish to share the season with."

Elizabeth's eyes danced. "Provided you do not cause too much trouble…such as getting arrested again!"

Richard grinned. "I will do my best, madam."

"We also have a wedding to plan." Elizabeth gave Georgiana a gentle smile.

His sister nodded. "Yes. But small, please."

"And soon," Richard interjected. They all laughed.

Elizabeth was so happy she seemed to sparkle; Darcy could not tear his eyes from her. "I am sorry all your search for a cottage will go to waste," she said to him.

"It need not," he replied. "We could stay at Pemberley until Twelfth Night and then spend a week on the shores of the lake."

"Just the two of us?" she asked.

"Indeed," he affirmed and could not restrain his need to give her a quick kiss.

Richard sighed and rolled his eyes dramatically. "We are *still* in the room!"

Elizabeth ignored his cousin. "That sounds lovely."

"And I shall stay at Pemberley to keep Georgiana company," Richard announced

Darcy narrowed his eyes at his cousin. "We still have Mrs. Annesley to fill that role—until you are married."

Richard scowled. "This is why it is imperative to have the wedding as soon as can be arranged."

Everyone laughed.

His cousin looked at Georgiana. "May I escort you to your room?" She gave him a shy nod, and they hurried away.

Darcy cleared his throat. "One more thing, Elizabeth." She gazed up at him with a trace of apprehension in her eyes. He removed something from his pocket and showed it to her. "I have been carrying this for more than a day in the hopes of having an opportunity to use it. Is now the moment?"

She smiled at the sight of a mistletoe berry in his palm. "I think now would be perfect."

Darcy pulled his wife to him with a gentle tug and claimed his prize.

Chapter Twenty One

Georgiana and Richard left Elizabeth and William making cow eyes at each other and headed for the stairs. Before they reached the bottom step, however, Richard said, "Could I beg a moment of your time before we retire for the night?"

"Of course." Georgiana experienced misgivings about the solemnity in his tone, but she changed direction, leading him out of the hall to the library.

"The library?" Richard asked in a low voice.

Georgiana shrugged. "No one is likely to visit it at this time of day." They slipped into the room, and she closed the door behind them. Richard lit two lamps, banishing the darkness with a soft, yellow glow.

Why was his manner suddenly so sober? Was something amiss? She bit her bottom lip as she considered what it could be.

"What is the matter, darling?" he asked.

"Are you truly angry with me for riding to Matlock?"

He sighed and rested his hands on her shoulders, a reassuring weight. "It was a very clever and brave thing to do, Georgiana. I am very touched by your concern and your devotion. But there are so many dangers for a woman riding through the countryside alone. If anything had happened to you..." He squeezed his eyes closed as if what he imagined caused him physical pain. "I would much rather stay in prison than lose you. I do not know what I would do without you."

His murmured words brought tears to Georgiana's eyes. "I have no plans to do such a ride again if that reassures you."

He flashed a quick smile. "And I have no plans to make it necessary again."

One of his hands moved from her shoulder to the side of her neck. His fingers on her bare flesh was a shocking and unexpected sensation but not unwelcome. Her eyes fell closed.

"Before their carriage left for Matlock, I told my parents about the betrothal." His voice was low.

Georgiana's eyes flew open. "What did they say?"

"My father was so surprised that he could not speak for a full thirty seconds. Then he congratulated me, patted me on the shoulder, and growled that I better be selling my commission." Richard smiled at the memory. "You know how he is." Georgiana nodded. "His next thought was about which estate we might purchase in Derbyshire."

Georgiana laughed. "I am happy he does not disapprove."

"Of course not. No one could possibly disapprove of you, Georgie. They love you, you know." He put his arms around her waist and pulled her closer.

"What did your mother say?" she asked.

Richard's eyes had a distant look. "It was the strangest thing. She merely said, 'At last you two figured it out.'"

Georgiana's eyes widened. "She knew we—"

"Apparently," Richard said.

Georgiana shook her head in disbelief.

Richard slid his other hand to the other side of her neck, warming it with the heat of his palm. "I am very happy to be free from jail for many reasons, but there is one reason above all."

"What is that?" Georgiana asked, a bit breathlessly.

"So I can do this." He pressed her against the door, leaning his body weight against hers.

As he kissed her, his hands thrust into her hair, bringing down her coiffure in a cascade of hairpins. He released her mouth, combing his fingers through her hair and spreading it over her shoulders. "I always wondered how it would look when it was down..."

"And how does it look?"

"Like liquid gold," he murmured and kissed her again.

Georgiana was helpless against the wave of tenderness that swamped her. She opened her mouth, savoring the way their tongues intertwined and dueled. His body was a welcome weight against hers, but she wanted more. Threading her fingers in his cravat, she pulled him closer until not a sliver of space separated their bodies at any point.

Her other hand plunged into his hair, pulling his head closer. She had expected to experience tenderness when she kissed him, but she was not prepared for the passion which seemed to sweep away all of her inhibitions.

"Oh, Georgiana," Richard groaned when they separated. "I hope this is a very short engagement." He trailed kisses down her neck to the place where her dress covered her shoulder. She shuddered with delight. "At this rate we will anticipate our marriage vows within a week."

"Richard!" Georgiana giggled, a little scandalized by his words.

He kissed his way up the other side of her neck. "Maybe"—kiss— "we could"—kiss—"marry"—kiss—"in a"—kiss—"month?"

With an effort of will, Georgiana dragged her attention back to the conversation. "Mrs. Annesley would believe that demonstrates undue haste."

Richard nuzzled her neck. "And what do you believe?"

"I believe it sounds perfect."

***

The moon shining off the water provided just enough illumination that Elizabeth could discern the contours of the lake and the trees on the surrounding shore. In the dead of winter Rudyard Lake at night was almost silent. There was nothing but the faint lapping of the water on the shore and an occasional rustle of leaves as the wind passed through the trees. The weather had continued mild, and she was quite comfortable standing on the cottage's porch with only a shawl over her dressing gown. Her mother would have had a fit of nerves if she saw Elizabeth outside in such clothing, but there was only one other person around for miles.

Swathed in his banyan, William stepped onto the porch, closing the cottage door with a soft click. "How lovely." He stood behind Elizabeth and wrapped his arms around her shoulders.

"Yes, I could watch it all night."

One of his hands massaged her neck, and she leaned back into the warm, welcoming sensation.

"This is the perfect antidote to a houseful of relatives," he murmured.

"We have relatives?" she asked.

He chuckled. "Perhaps next Christmas season we shall come here, and tell no one where we have gone."

"I like that plan." She leaned further into his embrace.

He stroked the hair that tumbled around her shoulders. "Elizabeth, please know that marrying you was the greatest, best, wisest decision I have ever made in my life." Tears immediately welled up in her eyes. "Nothing that could happen or that your family could do would ever change that."

How had he known the exact right thing to say? Elizabeth was so full of feeling that she could barely speak. She swallowed the lump in her throat. "What about something I do not do?"

William turned her around so he could look her in the eye, but she immediately hung her head. "What do you mean?" he asked.

"I have not quickened. I have not provided an heir for Pemberley." Despite her best efforts, her voice cracked on the last word.

William's face crumpled, and he pulled her into a tight embrace. "Dearest! Has that been weighing upon you?" Elizabeth nodded against his coat. "Oh, Elizabeth, I have been *pleased* that we did not have a child yet."

She pulled her head from his grasp to gape at him.

"It has been so thrilling having these months alone with just you…getting to know you… enjoying your company. I will welcome a child when we are blessed with one, but for now I am quite sufficiently blessed."

Elizabeth sagged in his arms. "Oh, thank goodness! I thought—!"

"I was displeased about the lack of an heir?" She nodded. "It will happen when the time is right, dearest." He waggled his eyebrows at her. "Perhaps tonight."

"Tonight?" She gave him an innocent expression. "Whatever do you mean?"

"Tonight," he insisted. "Right here."

"Here?" She scanned the porch and the surrounding wilderness.

"There is nobody to see us." He gave her a wicked smile that she had never before seen. "And you are so…" His hand reached out to untie one of the bows holding her dressing gown closed. "So beautiful in the moonlight. I do not believe I could make it back to the bedroom."

His other hand clasped the side of her neck and tilted up her chin. The faint moonlight illuminated his lips, luscious and tempting, descending toward hers. "Oh, Mr. Darcy…"

Epilogue

While December had been mild, January was quite cold—although Darcy teased his cousin that he could not possibly feel the chill with the glow of love illuminating him. Richard was far too happy to take offense.

Selecting a date for the wedding had not been difficult; Georgiana had wanted to be married after her eighteenth birthday, which occurred near the end of January. So they settled on a date a week after. However, choosing a venue for the wedding had been a point of contention between Richard and Georgiana on one side—who favored Pemberley—and Richard's parents on the other—who had offered Edgemont to host the event. There had been many polite but firm discussions without any resolution, until Georgiana received a letter from Lady Catherine announcing that if the wedding were to be held at Pemberley she would not attend "under any circumstances."

That instantly decided the question in favor of Pemberley. Even the earl and countess did not object; Lady Catherine had been their houseguest many times. Georgiana made a special visit to the kitchen to thank the staff again for their very good care of Lady Catherine.

Elizabeth also received a letter from Lydia expressing her regret that the Wickhams would be unable to attend the wedding.

On the day of the wedding, Elizabeth was dressed and ready far earlier than Darcy, who had fretted uncharacteristically over which waistcoat to wear. As he buttoned and tugged at his sleeves, Elizabeth read Lydia's letter aloud. Darcy's eyebrows shot upward. "You invited them to the wedding?"

"I most certainly did not," Elizabeth said.

After they enjoyed a good laugh, Elizabeth related Lydia's other piece of news. "She is in a family way. I supposed that explains why she nearly ate us out of house and home."

"Hmm. I suppose," Darcy said. "But I pray you do not invite her to visit until after the babe is born. I have grown to appreciate a steady supply of marmalade."

Elizabeth reassured her husband that she had no immediate plans to invite her sister to Pemberley. "Unfortunately," she observed, "that does not preclude her from visiting."

When Darcy had finished dressing, Elizabeth took his arm, and they strolled toward the stairs. As they walked, she told him about a letter from her father extolling the virtues of Scotland. "You may never persuade them to leave," she teased her husband.

He chuckled. "They are welcome to stay as long as your mother fears a French invasion." *Better there than here.*

"Or the war ends," Elizabeth observed.

"Perhaps we may visit them in the spring?" Darcy suggested, gazing fondly down at his wife as they descended the stairs. Their wedding trip had been delightful, and he would enjoy traveling with her again.

"I would like that," she said simply. "I have never seen Scotland."

They continued through the marble hall, which had already undergone a transformation with the addition of tapestries on the walls. Elizabeth had other plans to make the room more welcoming, but she had not yet revealed them to Darcy.

Soon they arrived at Pemberley's family chapel. Georgiana had insisted that they keep the wedding guest list small enough that they could hold the ceremony in the chapel rather than the local church. Darcy's wedding to Elizabeth had been far grander, but he delighted in the intimacy of Georgiana and Richard's day. Mrs. Reynolds had decorated the chapel simply in white flowers and ribbons, but the atmosphere was quite festive.

Many of the guests were already seated. Mr. and Mrs. Worthy were sitting in a far corner, exchanging besotted glances. Elizabeth had been quite triumphant when they were not only betrothed but married by Twelfth Night. However, nobody had been happier at the event than Mrs. Bracknell. Many of the other wedding guests were neighbors, and a few were friends of Georgiana's or Richard's. The bridegroom's parents were seated in the front row. Pemberley's servants occupied many of the back rows; Georgiana had insisted that they be included in her special day.

The ceremony was lovely. Darcy walked a radiant bride down the aisle and gave her hand into Richard's keeping. Elizabeth made copious use of her handkerchief throughout the service.

Afterward, everyone adjourned to the dining room for a wedding breakfast at Pemberley's new dining table. When Georgiana walked into the room, she gasped. The room's many windows gave a spectacular view of Pemberley's front lawn—now covered in an inch of thick snow.

"Oh, how lovely!" she exclaimed.

Richard grinned at the sight. "Perhaps we shall need to take a sleigh to Bellview." The small estate they had purchased was only a half hour from Pemberley.

"A sleigh!" Georgiana exclaimed. "It would be perfect."

Elizabeth and Darcy were standing next to the new husband and wife—also admiring the snow-covered vista. "I am looking forward to seeing Bellview," Elizabeth said.

Georgiana sighed. "It is beautiful."

"Not nearly as large as Pemberley," Richard said. "But that can be an advantage." Everyone turned questioning looks on him, even his new wife. "It has only two bedchambers for guests." He explained. "And I will take care that they are always occupied when Aunt Catherine is in the neighborhood."

Richard's reasoning evoked hearty laughter. Soon Elizabeth and Darcy drifted away to take their places at the table, but the newlywed couple remained to enjoy the view.

Richard took his new wife's hands and stood, mesmerized by her very presence—as they were silhouetted against the falling snow visible through the windows. He gave Georgiana a smile so full of love and tenderness that it was a miracle she did not melt into a puddle on the floor. "I hope you will be happy at Bellview."

Her eyes were suspiciously shiny as she regarded him. "I will be," she assured him. "It is perfect. Nobody has ever given me a better gift."

Richard lifted both of her hands to his lips. "But *I* have received a better gift." She gave him a quizzical look. "You agreed to be mine on Christmas day." He grinned.

"You are the best Christmas gift I ever received."

The End

Thank you for purchasing this book.

Your support makes it possible for authors like me to continue writing.

Please consider leaving a review where you purchased the book.

Learn more about me and my upcoming releases:

Sign up for my newsletter *Dispatches from Pemberley*

Website: www.victoriakincaid.com

Twitter: VictoriaKincaid@kincaidvic

Blog: https://kincaidvictoria.wordpress.com/

Facebook: https://www.facebook.com/kincaidvictoria

About Victoria Kincaid

The author of numerous best-selling *Pride and Prejudice* variations, historical romance writer Victoria Kincaid has a Ph.D. in English literature and runs a small business, er, household with two children, a hyperactive dog, an overly affectionate cat, and a husband who is not threatened by Mr. Darcy. They live near Washington DC, where the inhabitants occasionally stop talking about politics long enough to complain about the traffic.

On weekdays she is a freelance writer/editor who now specializes in IT marketing (it's more interesting than it sounds). In the past, some of her more…unusual writing subjects have included space toilets, taxi services, laser gynecology, bidets, orthopedic shoes, generating energy from onions, Ferrari rental car services, and vampire face lifts (she swears she is not making any of this up). A lifelong Austen fan, Victoria has read more Jane Austen variations and sequels than she can count – and confesses to an extreme partiality for the Colin Firth version of *Pride and Prejudice*.

Victoria Kincaid's Other Books

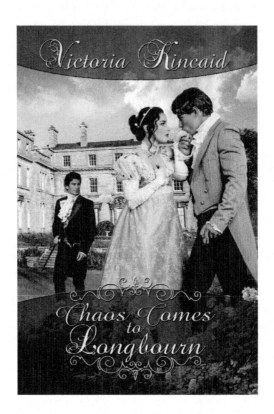

Chaos Comes to Longbourn

While attempting to suppress his desire to dance with Elizabeth Bennet, Mr. Darcy flees the Netherfield ballroom only to stumble upon a half-dressed Lydia Bennet in the library. When they are discovered in this compromising position by a shrieking Mrs. Bennet, it triggers a humorously improbable series of events. After the dust settles, eight of Jane Austen's characters are engaged to the wrong person.

Although Darcy yearns for Elizabeth, and she has developed feelings for the master of Pemberley, they are bound by promises to others. How can Darcy and Elizabeth unravel this tangle of hilariously misbegotten betrothals and reach their happily ever after?

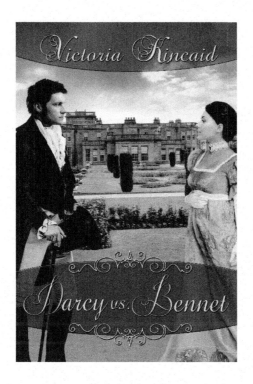

Darcy vs. Bennet

Elizabeth Bennet is drawn to a handsome, mysterious man she meets at a masquerade ball. However, she gives up all hope for a future with him when she learns he is the son of George Darcy, the man who ruined her father's life. Despite her father's demand that she avoid the younger Darcy, when he appears in Hertfordshire Elizabeth cannot stop thinking about him, or seeking him out, or welcoming his kisses....

Fitzwilliam Darcy has struggled to carve out a life independent from his father's vindictive temperament and domineering ways, although the elder Darcy still controls the purse strings. After meeting Elizabeth Bennet, Darcy cannot imagine marrying anyone else, even though his father despises her family. More than anything he wants to make her his wife, but doing so would mean sacrificing everything else....

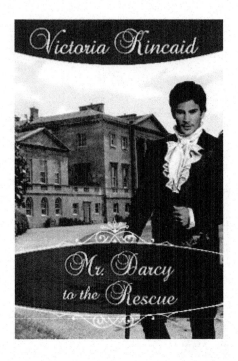

Mr. Darcy to the Rescue

When the irritating Mr. Collins proposes marriage, Elizabeth Bennet is prepared to refuse him, but then she learns that her father is ill. If Mr. Bennet dies, Collins will inherit Longbourn and her family will have nowhere to go. Elizabeth accepts the proposal, telling herself she can be content as long as her family is secure. If only she weren't dreading the approaching wedding day…

Ever since leaving Hertfordshire, Mr. Darcy has been trying to forget his inconvenient attraction to Elizabeth. News of her betrothal forces him to realize how devastating it would be to lose her. He arrives at Longbourn intending to prevent the marriage, but discovers Elizabeth's real opinion about his character. Then Darcy recognizes his true dilemma…

How can he rescue her when she doesn't want him to?

Pride and Proposals

What if Mr. Darcy's proposal was too late?

Darcy has been bewitched by Elizabeth Bennet since he met her in Hertfordshire. He can no longer fight this overwhelming attraction and must admit he is hopelessly in love. During Elizabeth's visit to Kent she has been forced to endure the company of the difficult and disapproving Mr. Darcy, but she has enjoyed making the acquaintance of his affable cousin, Colonel Fitzwilliam.

Finally resolved, Darcy arrives at Hunsford Parsonage prepared to propose—only to discover that Elizabeth has just accepted a proposal from the Colonel, Darcy's dearest friend in the world. As he watches the couple prepare for a lifetime together, Darcy vows never to speak of what is in his heart. Elizabeth has reason to dislike Darcy, but finds that he haunts her thoughts and stirs her emotions in strange ways.

Can Darcy and Elizabeth find their happily ever after?

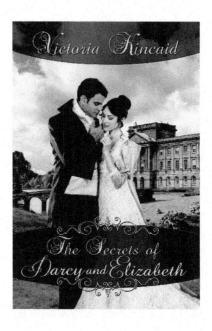

The Secrets of Darcy and Elizabeth

In this *Pride and Prejudice* variation, a despondent Darcy travels to Paris in the hopes of forgetting the disastrous proposal at Hunsford. Paris is teeming with English visitors during a brief moment of peace in the Napoleonic Wars, but Darcy's spirits don't lift until he attends a ball and unexpectedly encounters...Elizabeth Bennet! Darcy seizes the opportunity to correct misunderstandings and initiate a courtship.

Their moment of peace is interrupted by the news that England has again declared war on France, and hundreds of English travelers must flee Paris immediately. Circumstances force Darcy and Elizabeth to escape on their own, despite the risk to her reputation. Even as they face dangers from street gangs and French soldiers, romantic feelings blossom during their flight to the coast. But then Elizabeth falls ill, and the French are arresting all the English men they can find....

When Elizabeth and Darcy finally return to England, their relationship has changed, and they face new crises. However, they have secrets they must conceal—even from their own families.

When Mary Met the Colonel

Without the beauty and wit of the older Bennet sisters or the liveliness of the younger, Mary is the Bennet sister most often overlooked. She has resigned herself to a life of loneliness, alleviated only by music and the occasional book of military history.

Colonel Fitzwilliam finds himself envying his friends who are marrying wonderful women while he only attracts empty-headed flirts. He longs for a caring, well-informed woman who will see the man beneath the uniform.

A chance meeting in Longbourn's garden during Darcy and Elizabeth's wedding breakfast kindles an attraction between Mary and the Colonel. However, the Colonel cannot act on these feelings since he must wed an heiress. He returns to war, although Mary finds she cannot easily forget him.

Is happily ever after possible after Mary meets the Colonel?

CPSIA information can be obtained
at www.ICGtesting.com
Printed in the USA
LVOW13s1738251117
557538LV00034B/1379/P